I0578914

ALSO BY EDITH SCHEFFER

The Janie Chronicles

Saving Janie

Janie a Broad

Janie on Board

Janie vs. The Big Apple

* * *

Fallen Gracefully

* * *

Winged

Fallen Gracefully

EDITH SCHEFFER

FALLEN GRACEFULLY
ISBN 978-1-954174-21-4
Copyright © 2020 by Edith L. Scheffer
All rights reserved.
Edited by Louise Zanotto
Cover Art Design © 2020 by Croco Designs

This book is a work of fiction. The names, characters, places and incidents are products of the writers' imagination or have been used factiously and are not to be construed as real. Any resemblance to persons, living or dead, actual events, locale or organizations is entirely coincidental.

All rights are reserved. No part of this book may be used or reproduced in any manner whatsoever without written permission except in the case of brief quotations embodied in critical articles and reviews.

CHAPTER 1

FALLEN GRACEFULLY

No one wakes up and says, "I'm going to die today!" Let me reiterate: aside from suicide victims, no one wakes up and says that.

I did my morning routine: Coffee, workout for an hour (which is actually just dancing like a mad woman), shower, dress and off to work I go. It's been this way since I moved to Clackamas, Oregon a year ago.

I'm a massage therapist, so my days are filled with pulled hamstrings, pinched nerves, piriformis syndrome and sciatic issues. For seven hours a day, five days a week, I do my best to relieve other people's pain and help them relax.

Then, I head home in a car that just barely made it into the 21st century, to change into jammies, crack a beer, and sit outside on my third-story balcony. The sounds of the city are muted here as I enjoy a cold one and look at the stars.

If I'm hungry I grab something which usually consists of cheese and multigrain crackers, since I live alone. A few beers later I head to bed to start the day over again with the next sunrise. In all truthfulness I lead a boring life; not that I mind much.

Tomorrow I would wake up, make coffee, dance, shower, dress and head to work like always. But tomorrow would be a little different. At the end of tomorrow, I would be on vacation for a whole week. I could go home for a few days?

Just an hour from here is the small country town that claims me as one of their own. Mom, Dad, my sister and her family still live there. So does my lifelong best friend, Kris, short for Kristina. But if you were a friend you knew better than to call her by her Christian name. She would sooner respond to "Bitch." Not in a good way, but she would respond at least.

Truth was I missed everyone. I missed home. Now all I had to do was decide if I missed being home more than I wanted to avoid my ex-husband and the woman he had been screwing during our five year marriage. Hard choices required another beer.

I hadn't dated, not even once since the divorce. In all honesty, this one had done some damage. Aside from the wreck it made of my self esteem, it also gave me some trust issues. Even if those weren't in the forefront of my brain, I just couldn't even handle the thought of all that *getting to know you*, stuff. But in my case, heartbreak was always good for the waistline. I had dropped the ten pounds I had wanted to lose for the last two years. Twelve to be exact. Maybe it wasn't heartbreak that trimmed my waistline, I thought, patting my nonexistent stomach. Maybe it was not having mom constantly stuffing me with meat and potatoes. I smiled to no one. The woman was a great cook and I missed her.

Just then, the phone rang. "Hi mom," I answered.

"Hi my girl," rang back through the receiver. "How are you?"

"I'm good. How's you?" (Family talk)

"Not too bad. Made a few batches of chocolate chip cookies...just in case."

"Ah sweet bribery," I laughed.

"Is it gonna work this time?" she questioned.

I let out a sigh.

"So that's a no?" she asked.

"I'm still not sure," I admitted.

"Honey, I know it's hard for you, but it's been a year."

"I know mama. It's just so weird facing everyone. Knowing they all knew. Damn near everyone...but me, that is," I laughed.

"You couldn't have expected them to tell you?"

"I didn't. Really, I didn't. It wouldn't have been their place. It's just so...humiliating. I mean, I had her redecorate our house. The one she's now living in with my ex-husband. I just don't think I'm ready yet."

"I understand. Either way, I'll be coming to your place next month to get my Gracie fill."

I smiled, "I can't wait. I made us pedicure appointments at *Touche*."

"Oh I love Portland. Speaking of Portland..."

I took a draw of my beer, here it comes, I thought.

"Have you met anyone?" mom asked.

"Since I talked to you three days ago? No."

"It's just...someone out there...deserves someone like you," mom said.

"Well then, he's gonna have to find me," I laughed again.

"Well, that's what I pray for at night."

"Well, with you praying it's bound to happen, mama."

"I better go wake your father from his easy chair and coax him to bed. I love you, Gracie girl."

"I love you too, mama." I hung up the phone and let out a deep sigh.

The moon was starting to dip when I finished my beer and headed to bed.

I woke from a dreamless sleep, pulled my long blond hair into a ponytail and did my morning ritual. While I brushed my teeth, I noticed that my right shoulder was a little stiff. I mentally went over which L.M.T. I would have work on me. I decided on Greg for arm and shoulder work. But that would have to wait, seeing as how all of our therapists were booked out weeks in advance.

When I opened my front door, a small box was staring at me from my doorstep. Leaning down, I realized it was for the man on the second floor. This happened often enough that I wasn't surprised. He spent a great deal of time out of the country on business. He had asked if I would mind babysitting the packages until he returned home.

I carried the package down one flight to his apartment, and gave his door a rap. I waited a moment with no answer, so I carried it back up to my apartment and placed it safely inside under my claw footed couch. Out of sight, out of mind, I thought to myself. I would catch him later when he returned home from God knows where.

He was a nice man, in his late fifty's, I imagined. Russian, I think. His accent was beautiful, even if it did make me think of Boris and Natasha from the Rocky and Bullwinkle cartoons. His hair showed no sign of thinning, although the salt and pepper *do* had more salt than pepper. He was about my height, 5'9" I'd guess. Impeccably dressed, he always wore slacks and a button down shirt topped off with a blazer, a very expensive looking watch and wing tips. I wasn't sure what he did for a living, but he dressed far above the standards of what our rent would indicate. But not everyone who made good money needed to live in a mansion.

I drove two miles away and pulled into my usual spot. I waited for our desk girl, Emily, to arrive and unlock the doors.

In my private room; I lit my candles, made sure I had enough lotion in my bottle and turned on the towel warmer. I was ready for the day.

I had three one hour appointments before lunch and was ready for a rest. Sitting in the break room, I ate the cheese, crackers and grapes I had brought from home.

Annie came in for her lunch break as well. She was a little shorter than me, with a smile that transformed her and made her green eyes sparkle in her caramel face.

"Hey, I forgot you worked today," she smiled at me. "I thought you were on vacation?"

"Starts tonight," I smiled back.

"So, are you going home for your vacation?" her brows arched.

I shook my head, "Not really sure yet."

She gave me the sad eyes, "You should do something with your time off. Do you have any plans?"

"No. I think I may just stay home. Do some spring-cleaning. Relax."

"It's winter, Gracie. You need to get out. Would you like to come with me and the girls tonight? There's a bar in downtown we're all dying to check out. We're going to have expensive cocktails and sing karaoke."

Laughing, I shook my head again, "Not really my thing. But thank you for the invite."

"You're always invited!" her eyes rounded at me. "Just once, it would be nice if you accepted."

"It's not you guys, it's me."

"Are you really giving me the, *it's not you it's me*, speech?" she laughed.

I laughed back and threw a towel at her, "Well, it is me."

I had two more appointments to go; each of them an hour and a half. After the first, I was informed that my last appointment had cancelled. Looking at my schedule, I nodded. It was Ms. Spicer. She was an eccentric, to say the least. Chances were that the stars weren't properly aligned for a visit today. Secretly, I was thrilled. I was ready to just go home, crack a beer, and put my feet up...possibly for a whole week.

I said my goodbyes, after I put my name down on Greg's book for the week after next. In my car I remembered that I was not only short on beer but toilet paper. Two things I didn't want to run out of...ever.

I drove passed my apartment complex to the grocery store a mile away. This was one of the few stores in the Portland area that hadn't been remodeled. It was now 70's chic.

My beer was on sale, a case for the price of a twelve pack. I decided that this was a good buy, considering it had no chance of going bad in my fridge. Next, I noticed that toilet paper was also on sale. But it was one ply. I wasn't even sure why they sold that, much less tried to pass it off as a great buy. I would pay the extra money for a little comfort. My big splurge.

Back at my apartment, I put the case under one arm, and grabbed the T.P. with the other. Up the two flights I went. I knocked on my downstairs neighbor's door and waited. Still no answer.

Picking up my case of beer, I climbed another flight and fought a little with my keys before finding the lock. I walked through my tiny living room and clicked on the kitchen light with my elbow as I passed. Putting the beer in my fridge, I noticed how devoid of food it looked and decided to order a pizza. Grabbing a beer, I twisted the top off and took a long much needed and wanted pull off the bottle.

When I set my beer down...a hand cupped my mouth. Another arm wrapped around my waist. I grabbed for the beer to use as a weapon but it was just out of reach. I tried to throw my head back in an attempt to break the nose of whoever had me but I hit his chest. I tried to kick his legs, stomp his foot and bite the hand covering my mouth, all to no avail. I was being dragged backward down my hallway to my bedroom.

I'd love to say that I remained calm. But that wasn't really on my agenda as the picture in my head was me raped then killed on my bed. Police would come to examine my apartment, take my beer and use my toilet paper. My legs flailed as I tried to break something, make enough noise to concern my neighbors. It also popped into my head that my Russian neighbor wasn't home apparently. And the woman on the first floor was practically deaf. I kicked my dresser hard and felt immediate pain in my heel.

"You're gonna hurt yourself!" said the deep voice from behind me. "Stop!"

I stopped for a moment to wonder; why would a thief, rapist, murderer, care if I hurt myself? I pondered this then returned to trying to bite his hand while flailing my body as best I could. I refused to give up easily. If I was going out, I was going to make it the worst experience of his life, too. And maybe leave some telltale sign of who it was that did whatever this freak planned on doing to me. I got my body turned just enough that I got one arm free. That hand balled into a fist and punched him square in the ball-sack. I heard him squeak, as he quickly re-pinned my arm to my side.

"Oh...my..." he breathed, resting his head on my shoulder. I lifted my good heel and stomped down hard on his foot with my Doc Marten Mary Jane's. This had the less desired effect of him falling on me. To the bed we went face down, with him on top of me. The tables not well in my favor to begin with, had taken a turn for the *even worse.*

He was heavy on me and I was already having trouble breathing, considering how frightened I was. I got my other arm unpinned and threw an elbow backward, which hit him in the ribs. This forced the air from his lungs. Then I felt my other wrist being pulled up. I heard click, as one hand was cuffed to my headboard.

Handcuffs? Really? Do most rapists bring cuffs? What kind of kinky murderous freak was he?

He was still lying across me, holding my mouth with his other hand.

"Don't fight. Don't yell. I don't want to have to gag you."

Those words...scared the hell out of me. I was already having trouble breathing. Gagged would not make this feat any easier.

"I'm not gonna hurt you!" said the deep, out of breath voice.

This brought no comfort as I assumed anyone who thought breaking into your home and raping you, wasn't considered hurtful. He was undoubtedly certifiable. Maybe he wasn't going to rape me? Maybe he was a thief? The more I rolled this thought around in my head, the more I felt kind of sorry for a would-be thief that would try robbing me. I had just short of nothing: An old TV? An old wedding ring I hadn't had the heart to sell. Not because I was sentimental about the damned thing, but because I thought it contained bad juju and I was reluctant to pass it on to someone else. I had a laptop that held the same ranking as my car; Old, beat up and the drive barely worked. And again, what thief brought handcuffs?

"Tell me you won't scream!" he said, pulling me from my thoughts.

How the hell could I tell him...anything? Finally, I just nodded in agreement.

"Are you nodding that you will be quiet, or not?"

I stopped and tried to look back at him with a much furrowed brow. Was he kidding me? I huffed through his hand as he rephrased the question.

"Will you be quiet?"

I nodded. He wasn't asking me for a promise or a *pinky swear*? Not a very smart would-be thief, rapist, murderer, if you ask me. Everyone knows an agreement isn't promised until a pinky is involved.

He removed his hand cautiously and I took a few much needed deep breaths. Slowly, I felt his body remove its weight from mine. My lungs felt like they might once again fill with air. Now I had a new problem. I was panic breathing. I was getting dizzy. What little light from the kitchen that made its way into my room was being shrunk by blackness. I was going to pass out...and did.

CHAPTER 2

A DIFFERENT POINT OF VIEW...FROM ERNIE

"Are you spying on that woman again?" Ernie asked as he set down their takeout bag of greasy burgers and fries.

"Knushka isn't home. Or I'd be spying on him," he answered, looking through binoculars.

"Yeah. Sure you would," Ernie said sarcastically. "Come on and eat while it's still a mushy mess of preservatives and heart clogging fat."

"I forgot how much fun you are on a stakeout," he grinned. "Now you're gonna tell me you miss your wife?"

"Not exactly," said Ernie looking at his flat burger. "I miss her cooking, though," he took a bite like he was afraid of being poisoned.

"This hasn't even been the longest stakeout we've been on."

"True, but I'm not a young man anymore," he dabbed his rain drenched balding skull with a napkin. "This shit's getting old. It's making me old."

His partner laughed, "Yeah, I can see that."

"You know this job isn't healthy to begin with, but you mooning over some unsuspecting woman...it's a little creepy," Ernie nodded.

"I have a wire tap, signed by a judge, it's all legal."

"Yeah. But you got that wire tap due to some serious fudging of her possible involvement," Ernie made air quotes with his fingers.

"What?" he put his hands up innocently. "Knushka's out of the country a lot and the packages ARE being delivered to her. Who knows what her connection is?" he grinned.

"You know!" Ernie shook his head. "You know that she…"

"Shhh, she's getting a call!" There was a moment of silence. "It's her mom."

"No kiddin'," Ernie said, feigning surprise as he went back to his meal.

Ernie's partner listened to the whole taped conversation. "She just seems so...sweet."

"Yeah," Ernie said, throwing wilting fries into his mouth. "You know, you're a good looking guy."

"Uh, thanks man, but you know my boat doesn't float that way," he smiled.

"Right. Anyway, you have women falling at your feet. What the hell are you doing mooning over a woman who doesn't even know you exist? It's just...wrong. I could be living vicariously through you and that aerobics instructor. What was her name again?" he scratched his head.

"Cindy with an 'I'?" his partner said stretching out his long legs and locking his fingers behind his head.

"Yeah, Cindi. She was hot."

"Yeah. But that's all she was. She was as boring as this burger," he said, checking out his own squished dinner. "She had no substance and couldn't talk about anything but working out."

"I bet she was fun in the sack, though!" Ernie raised a brow.

"It's not much fun to spend the next twenty-three hours with someone who can't hold a conversation, that doesn't include supplements or fat intake."

"An hour?" Ernie looked off into space. "Yeah, you aren't married."

"She wasn't the one," his partner said, shaking his head.

"Ah, come on, Fall, for me?" Ernie asked making puppy dog eyes.

CHAPTER 3

ENTER THE FALL

The next morning, I watched her on her balcony. She sipped her coffee as the sun rose. And after a good stretch, that I thoroughly enjoyed watching, she disappeared back into the house to get ready for her day. At 7am I saw the UPS truck round her building. I strolled outside wearing a baseball cap and sunglasses.

As I rounded her building I could see a package had been set on her door step. I waited for the UPS driver to leave and then cautiously I climbed the stairs to check the *deliver to* name. It was Knushka. Back down the stairs I went. Knushka's black BMW hadn't been in his parking space for days. But I knew...with the arrival of this package, it was only a matter of time.

I had to go into the office sometime today. Even with the invention of E-mail, I still didn't like sending private information over the net even if it was a secure system. I wasn't sure what Knushka was capable of, but I didn't put anything past him or his desire to stay invisible.

Sitting at my desk, I wrote the weekly report. It was really more of an update which contained no change since last week's update. After this, I ran to the grocery store to see if I could find something to make Ernie for dinner, that wouldn't harden his arteries. I was poking around the produce section when Ernie called.

"Hey, I was walking the grounds and someone just went into your girlfriend's apartment...I think."

"Who? Was in Knushka?"

"I didn't get a good look. He was wearing a jacket and a wide brimmed hat. Same height as Knushka...looked older like Knushka."

Out of the store I bolted and jumped in my '68 Charger. The tires squealed as I turned out of the lot and headed to the complex. I had to park by our apartment to keep nosey eyes from spying me.

I skirted the building and saw a man who very well could have been the person Ernie had seen. He walked to a maroon Pathfinder and put a package in his passenger seat. He didn't even seem to notice me as he got into the driver's side and slowly rolled away. I took down the make and model of the vehicle and the license number before I headed up the stairs.

The package was gone. But chances were Grace had taken it inside for safe keeping. But this guy, whoever he was, had been in her apartment? Was the package he had the one we were waiting for? Knushka wasn't known for leaving loose ends. Even though we had never been able to directly connect him to anything, lots of his *associates* wound up six feet under, or other colorful ways of dead. One guy was found strung up like a marionette. He looked as though he was doing a morbid dance animated by the frayed electrical cords that held his arms and legs. This was my biggest fear for Grace. She had no idea that by housing his packages she had made herself a complication that would need to be taken care of.

I pulled out my lock picks and worked quickly. The door

sprung open. I entered and immediately closed and locked the door behind me.

This was Grace's house. I took a deep breath and could smell a hint of vanilla. I loved that scent. From our second story apartment, I couldn't really see much of hers. Everything I knew about her was from a wire tap and watching her on her balcony. It was what I expected though; sparse, but comfortable. She even had a fireplace. Everything was clean and put away. No clutter, really. A few pictures of what I assume must be her family, her best friend and her best friend's husband, sat on a desk that butted up to her window. I started to look for the package. It wasn't in plain view, if it was here at all. Not in her living room, kitchen, bathroom. I even looked in her clothes washing nook/hall closet. Nothing. I decided to look in her bedroom.

Down the hall I went, feeling more like a stalker than I wanted to. She had a small all in one TV/DVD player on her night table, a dresser, a full sized bed with a very plain wrought iron barred headboard and green quilted comforter with tiny little yellow flowers. No junk, no throw pillows, and only one stuffed bear that I assumed held some sentimental significance. I looked in her walk-in closet; it was clean and only half full. Not a clothes horse or shoe junkie, I see. She had a basket with a lid that contained old pictures, letters and private things that I had no right to look through. Although...I was tempted.

My phone rang and it jolted me back to reality.

"Hey! Your girlfriend's home! You may wanna get the hell out of there!" Ernie said.

"She's not supposed to be home for an hour!" I said, wondering what the hell to do.

"Well, I don't know what to tell ya, Cinderella's home. Where are you?"

"Uhhh."

"Are you fuckin' kiddin' me?" Ernie asked. "Are you IN her apartment?"

"Well...yeah."

"Why the hell did you go in her apartment?" I could almost picture that vein in Ernie's head, threatening to pop.

"I needed to see if the package was still here!"

"Shit, shit, shit! This is gonna cost us the case, if not our badges! What are you gonna do?"

"I'll think of something. She's here. Gotta go."

I clicked off the phone and hall light, while Ernie was still in full cuss mode. I saw her pass into the kitchen, arms full. There was no way in this small apartment, I could hide successfully. I couldn't fit under the bed. If she opened the closet, I'd be in plain view. Not enough clothes to hide me. Maybe, if I was really quiet, I could sneak out the front door.

I walked down the hall, pushing myself against the wall. Peeking around the corner, I saw her in her fridge. She was faced in my direction. When I looked again, she had her back to me, cracking open a beer. I figured I'd sneak out while she took a drink but then she set the beer down and was beginning to turn. Without thinking, I grabbed her.

One arm went around her waist, holding her arms at her sides. The other hand covered her mouth. I had no idea what to do, so I pulled her back to her room, but now what? Do I tell her who I am? That could put her in more danger. She was flailing wildly. Not the way I wanted to meet her. At least I knew how to hold her so neither of us would get hurt. We're taught exactly how to do this. That's what I was thinking, when she got a hand free and punched me square in the balls. I yelped and said, "Oh...my...!" but a masculine kind of yelp. She tried many times to bite my hand as I cupped her mouth. Still trying to get control of her free hand, she stomped hard on my foot. Between that and the ball racking I had taken, I fell to the bed with her beneath me. I tried to catch my breath without squishing her. Her other arm worked free and she threw her elbow backwards into my ribs, knocking what little wind I had regained, back out of me. I didn't know what else to do. This was like fighting a feral cat. Looks sweet, but will fuck you up. Finally, I reached in to my back pocket, grabbed my cuffs and cuffed her other hand to the headboard. I still had a hand covering her mouth. "Are you gonna be quiet if I remove my hand?"

She nodded. I lifted my body off of hers, then took some deep breaths. So much for neither of us getting hurt. My balls felt like she had run a pool table with them. I looked down at her motionless body. She was out cold. Fainted. Yep, definitely not the way I wanted to meet her. I found a washcloth in her hall closet and wet it down. Placing it on her forehead, she let out a moan. I was already smitten with her.

I found a zip-lock bag in a drawer in the kitchen and filled it with ice from her almost empty freezer. Shoving it down my pants, I took in a deep breath as the cold hit my sack.

"It's okay guys," I said to them. "We've been through worse."

Dialing Ernie's number, the first words out of his mouth were, "What the hell have you done?"

I explained what happened. I expected no sympathy for my racked sack, bruised foot and ribs, and received none.

"You really blew the shit out of this one, Fall! What are you gonna do now? Just leave? Leave her cuffed? Go uncuff her and risk her seeing you?" Ernie was just as full of bad ideas as I was.

"I'll think of something," I told him.

"Oh, since you put it that way, I feel a lot better. Since your last *I'll think of something*, went so fuckin' well."

"I'll call you in the morning," I said.

"In the morning?" Ernie yelled.

Truthfully, I didn't know what to do. Knushka was a dangerous man. Adding to his cut-throat-style was a deep-seated sense of paranoia. If he did talk to her and she showed any fear or change in personality, he would assume something was amiss and resolve the situation without haste. And even if she showed no change in personality he would never allow someone who could testify against him to live.

After coming up with no plan to fix my FUBAR, I went back into her room to check on her. She was still out, so I took the rag and rewetted it. As I placed it back on her forehead, I felt the overwhelming need to touch her face. She was such a beautiful woman. Not in that *looks beautiful all done up with a pint of makeup*, just naturally beautiful.

CHAPTER 4

I'M AWAKE

When I came too, my arm was still cuffed. It took me a moment to remember what had brought on this unconscious time warp. My forehead felt damp and I was worried that I had been struck and was going to bleed out. But when I reached a cautious hand to my brow, a dampened rag was there. No wounds that I could feel. Had the would-be murderer, rapist, thief, just up and left? And left me cuffed to my headboard, no less?

Just then, I heard him rifling through my kitchen cupboards. What was he looking for? Surely I had nothing in my kitchen he would want. I guess I had expensive cookware that the Ex and I had received as a wedding present. But I had never heard of a culinary thief. Quickly the child in me regretted not using my pots and pans more when I had the chance.

Maybe, he would steal the cookware and be on his way. I debated screaming. Certainly I had at least a moment or two of some good screams before he gagged me. The *gagging* part, made me feel woozy again. Better not risk it. Plus...who would hear me? It was a pretty big gamble not knowing if anyone would be alerted enough to come save me. And if no one came, I would have broken a promise to what must be a psycho and earned a rag stuffed in my mouth...or worse. I didn't want anything stuffed anywhere.

Just then, I heard him speaking to someone, "It's not like I planned it this way!" Then there was silence. Had he let someone else in my apartment? Had there always been another person here that I just didn't know about?

"She's fine," he said to no one.

Oh no. What if he's so crazy, and he THINKS someone else is here? Oh, how sad, I thought. Then I chastised myself for feeling sorry for the person who broke in my home, took me captive, handcuffed me, and was now stealing the best cookware made in the whole wide world.

"I'm not sure what I'll tell her, but there's not much else I can do. I'll think of something." Then there was silence, followed by, "I'll call you in the morning."

I was grateful to hear he had been on the phone, but with whom? The words "In the morning," finally hit my brain. He plans on leaving, but not until morning? I had hoped it would be sooner than that. Preferably after he uncuffed me, I prayed.

I saw his shadow and heard his footfall coming down the hall. Was I supposed to talk to him? Maybe I should pretend I'm still unconscious? I put the rag back on my head and feigned being out cold.

My room was so dark (thanks to blackout shades), that very little light made its way down the hallway from the kitchen to my bedroom. Through the small, hairline lift in the rag, I could see that he was tall. But I had already been under that assumption since my failed *nose breaking* attempt. He looked as though he was muscular. That was fine for most women, and in most cases, but in this particular situation...not so good for me.

"Grace?" he called.

This caught me off guard. How did he know my name? It was

harder to feign unconsciousness hearing him call me by name. My heart began to pound harder. I was certain I didn't know him. Of that, I was positive.

"Grace?" he reached out and grabbed the rag.

I held my eyes shut and kept up the pretense, willing my breath to slow and deep.

Off he went to my bathroom where the water was turned on. A moment later, he returned and put the newly wetted towel back on my head. I felt his hand caress my cheek. He pulled a blanket up over my body before he headed back into the kitchen.

W.T.H.? I wondered. Oh my GOD...was I to be...a pet? Or a captive doll of some kind? I could see a little down the hall from the back glow of the kitchen light. I watched him grab one of the quilts from the hall closet then he disappeared into the living room. He was going to sleep? With a woman cuffed to her headboard in the bedroom? I was now pretty sure...rapist, he was not.

A million thoughts turned in my head, most of them ending with the same conclusion. W.T.F.? Somewhere around 3am, much against my will, I fell asleep.

When I woke, the room was still dark thanks again to my blackout shades. Turning my head, my clock read 8am. I wondered if he had gone. I couldn't hear anything but my TV; sounded as though he was watching the news. Great, he's that guy. He was probably looking to see if the police were closing in on him; the would-be thief and murderer. Rapist was now off the list.

Just then, I heard noises from my kitchen. He was still here and was coming toward my room. I decided I couldn't fake sleep forever just hoping he would leave, so I hoisted my body up against my headboard with my one free arm. I was ready to confront him, cautiously.

He set something on my dresser and turned in my direction.

"You're awake? Good. How did you sleep?" he asked.

"Really?" I expelled, not expecting it to sound nearly as sarcastic as it had. "I slept cuffed to my headboard. How did you sleep?" I fired back.

"Yeah, sorry about that, your couch is a little short for me, so I slept on the floor."

I shook my head, "Why?"

"Like I said, the couch is a little short."

"No! I mean, why haven't you left? What are you going do with me?"

"Nothing," he said quickly, his palms flew up submissively like the thought shouldn't have even been a question.

There was a silence while I tried to figure out if this was my new life. He isn't going to do anything to me, yet, I'm still bound to my bed by what I can only assume is some kind of freak or psycho.

"So...are you leaving?" I asked.

"Well, I actually can't just yet. It's not safe."

"Not safe? Are you running from the police? Because I won't say a word about this! You just uncuff me, I'll count to...like a million and we can just pretend this never happened. I mean, I haven't seen your face...couldn't pick you out of a lineup if I wanted to...so, I mean, you have nothing to fear from me," I explained.

I could make out his shadow, nodding, "I'm aware," is all he said. Then he stood and grabbed a tray, setting it on my lap.

"What's this?"

"Breakfast," he told me.

"O-kay."

"You need to eat. I would've made you dinner last night, but you were out cold."

This thought rolled around in my head. Would have made me dinner? If he was murderer, did he have some kind of relationship fetish? I had seen something like this on CIS or CIA, one of those shows with initials. The guy had to live out a marriage fantasy, before he killed the woman. My heart began to beat hard.

"Um, I didn't have any food in my refrigerator. How'd you make breakfast?" I asked.

"Oh, I went to the store," he explained.

"You left...and left me cuffed to my headboard...then came back...with food?" my mind bending.

"Yeah, like you said, there was nothing in your fridge," he pointed out the logic behind his actions.

I wasn't a big fan of batshit crazy. "Okay, just exactly HOW am I supposed to eat?"

"What do you mean?" he asked.

I was becoming frustrated, "I mean, one arm is cuffed to my headboard and I can't see my plate, much less my food."

"I could feed you?" he suggested.

"I'd rather you didn't," I said matter-of-factly.

I saw his shadow nod again. "I get that. Okay, I'm going to turn on the light."

Great, now I WOULD be able to pick him out of a lineup.

"And the arm?" I asked.

He thought for a moment, "I'll uncuff you."

This is too weird, is what I was thinking when he stood and moved to the light switch.

"Okay. You ready? This may hurt your eyes a bit," he warned.

The light was clicked on and I squinted hard at the pupil change. When I finally opened them, there he stood: Tall. Very tall, six-four I would imagine. His dark hair was longer on top and fell in waves, a three day shadow beard over olive skin. His eyes were a deep brown, like dark chocolate. His white Hanes t-shirt clung to all the right sculpted places. His 501's hung around his hips and were well worn in more ways than one. My eyes softened with such a view. Noticing, he smiled and what a dazzling smile he had. I had to quickly remind myself, the devil came in a most appealing package.

I don't know what I had pictured in my head. Maybe more *Captain Spaulding* and less *Calvin Klein* model. My palms began to sweat. Somehow, he looked...familiar? Although, I couldn't for the life of me imagine from where. He wasn't a client. Not of mine, for sure. Was he another L.M.T.'s client? I never went...anywhere. I hadn't seen him in the building or at the pool that I had used twice in the last year. As I pondered, I looked down at my plate. This had my concern rising. It was exactly what I would have made if I had cooked myself breakfast. Eggs over medium, bacon crisp and sourdough bread with real butter. I could tell it was real butter without tasting it because it was white, not yellow. A small ramekin held raspberry jam, my favorite. There was no way this was a coincidence. Now I had another disturbing thought. Had this man, who knew my name, been watching me? Waiting for the right time to strike?

He moved to the other side of the bed and pulled a key from his pocket. I went deathly still as if one movement would make him change his mind. I heard the *clink* and realized I was free. I rubbed at my wrist, more for confirmation of freedom, than out of pain.

"Is your wrist okay?" he grabbed it and brought it up for inspection.

My brow furrowed, "Why do you care?" I asked without thinking. But after everything that had happened, all of my fears, concerns and questionings were coming to the surface.

He stammered, "I...I don't want to hurt you."

My mouth was the smallest of my problems as I rolled my eyes and let out a "Huh! How can you say that? I mean really, how can you say that?" It was over, my patience was gone. I was no longer polite and my nerves were shot.

He looked down and let out a sigh, like he had been wounded

by my statement. "I really didn't intend for things to go this way," he shook his head.

"What was the intended outcome of breaking into my home, attacking me, cuffing me, putting a cold rag on my head then making me breakfast?"

"So you were awake...when I put the rag on your head?"

"Of course I was awake. Scared shitless seems to affect my sleep pattern!"

"I didn't want to scare you. I just...it didn't work out the way I had planned," he shook his head.

"What the hell did you plan? Better yet, what are you planning to do now? Are you going to rape me?" I asked.

His face squished up, as I kept rambling.

"Murder me? Steal from me? What the hell is this?" I was losing it.

"I'm not a murderer," he began to laugh as he shook his head. "You don't have anything to steal. And for damn sure, I would never rape you."

Now I was slightly offended. He didn't have to point out that I had nothing to steal. I knew that. I just wasn't sure he did. And he wouldn't rape me? Does that mean he IS a rapist but wouldn't touch ME with a ten-foot-pole? "Oh yeah, and why wouldn't you rape me?" Why I asked was either ego driven or a walk down *stupidity lane*, as I'm sure I really didn't want to know.

"Because I'm not a rapist, either," he offered plainly.

"Why are you here?" my eyes widened.

"I can't tell you that...not yet."

I rolled my eyes.

"What I can tell you, is I'm not going to hurt you."

I met his eyes; mine filled with absolute disdain. What I saw in his was a combination of fear, pleading and longing.

"I want to tell you, I do, but not yet. It's not safe," his eyes bored into mine, begging me to try and understand.

With our eyes locked, he stared directly into mine. It almost had me convinced that he was being honest with me. Well, as honest as he could be without explaining anything.

"I have to pee," was all I could say.

He took the tray off my lap and escorted me to the bathroom.

"Are you going to stand outside the door and listen?" I asked.

"Do I have to?" he asked with a serious tone.

I pondered...this seemed like a logical question on his part, I guess. I shook my head no.

"You'll be good?"

Mentally I wondered what he thought I would do in a third story bathroom with no window. I nodded.

Into the bathroom I went, closing and locking the door behind me. I caught a glimpse of myself in the mirror. Hair, a long matted mess, mascara smeared, teeth that needed a good brushing. I peed, washed my face, brushed my teeth and took a deep breath. No, this was not a dream, I told myself. This was really happening. Trying to think of how I could get away from him...how I could make all of this, whatever it was, stop, I searched for a weapon. Toilet brush: flimsy dollar store brush that threatened to break when used for its intended purpose. I pictured myself wielding it and was more than sure this wouldn't help me. Razor; electric. I had succumbed to an infomercial about how this razor gently removed the hair from the follicle. I only still used the torture device because it cost a small fortune. It was heavy; I guess I could ding his skull with it. But I had the feeling this would just be taken away from me and I would be cuffed again, watching him manicure his shadow of a beard. If I had had Clorox bleach, I could squeeze it in his eyes and run. I began to quietly chastise myself for buying all this non-toxic cleanser so I could do my part to save the environment. I pictured squeezing a bottle of Green World cleaner at him and him *opening wide* to use it as mouth wash. Did I really have nothing in my bathroom that could assist me with saving myself? A pair of tweezers was all I found that could be used as a weapon. I stared at them and frowned. Not really the *Ninja* I'd need to be to make this work. My bathrobe, complete with tie, could be used to choke him...If I was bigger, stronger, and a little less circus clown, maybe.

"Um, you okay in there?" he asked through the door.

Pulled from my thoughts, I answered quickly in one word, "Yep-sure-why?"

"You've been in there for a half an hour. Do you need something? Is it...um...your time?"

My eyes bugged towards the closed door, "My time?" I repeated.

"Yeah, you know, your...time."

"Yeah, got it," I said quickly.

"Well, I don't want to be insensitive...and ya know...thought I should...ya know, ask?"

"Well you shouldn't," I let him know. "We don't have an intimate relationship," I said hotly. "So you shouldn't ask an intimate question!"

"I'm sorry, I just, ugh...," he trailed off. "I'm sorry," he said through the crack.

Totally without a desire to, I laughed. It was funny to hear him be so wonky with his hostage.

I shook my head and decided that nothing would be an effective weapon in my hands. Opening the door, he motioned me into the kitchen.

"I brought your breakfast in here. I figured that maybe you needed to get out of your room." When he said it, I realized this was actually a much needed change of scenery. Away from the bed, seemed like a good idea, even if he wasn't a rapist.

As I sat at my two-seater makeshift island/table, I could see out the window. It was a drizzly overcast day in the great Northwest.

The kind of day I loved, normally. And normally, I would have coffee, no breakfast, out on my balcony and enjoy the falling rain.

I watched him plating food. In front of me, he sat a newly cooked breakfast.

"You didn't have to do that," I said. "I would have eaten the other plate."

"No, it's cold. I'll eat that one. We need to get some warm food in you, especially since you didn't have dinner."

He poured me a cup of coffee. Now this was a weapon, I thought. I gave it some serious consideration. After watching how he had taken a direct hit to the sack, I wasn't gonna risk it. Plus, I really needed my coffee.

He grabbed the other plate and sat across from me. I was starving but waited for him to take the first bite. After all, if he was going to poison my food, he wouldn't eat from a plate that had been intended for me, right?

He dug in, as did I. It seemed weird. Not just the whole incident as it was but to have him eating at my table. Neither of us said anything, then all of the sudden he piped up. "Oh, you probably want the paper, don't you?"

"Um...sure," I responded, trying not to look as baffled as I felt.

He walked out of my small kitchen, through my small living room, and opened the front door. A moment later the morning news paper was sat beside my plate.

I bit my lower lip.

"I'm sorry, did you need more cream?" he asked.

I just shook my head. How, or why rather, would I tell a complete stranger (especially one who had broken into my home and taken me hostage), that I had never had a man wait on me before? Much less make a meal for me. Save for my dad alone, of course.

Five years of marriage and I had become the perfect slave. Even though I had a nine-to-five as a massage therapist, I also did all of the cooking, cleaning, laundry, errand running and bill paying. I had convinced myself that his job was so much more involved and stress filled than mine. I felt sorry for him when he would pull his exhausted self to the dinner table. Now I knew part of his exhaustion was probably from the two hour lunch dates where he boffed his mistress, not just from his long hours as a used car salesman. My captor was staring at me as I lost myself in thought.

"You okay?" he looked concerned.

"I'm just not used to being waited on," I finally said. "This is very good," I pointed to my plate. "Thank you," I added, not sure if I should thank him but knowing I had been raised to do so.

"I got the last jar of raspberry jam. I was lucky. Someone had shoved it behind the blackberry," he smiled.

I looked sidelong at him, "How did you know raspberry was my favorite?"

He looked caught off guard and pondered how to answer, "Just a guess," he said avoiding my eyes.

I opened the paper, wondering if his face would be splashed across the front page. Nope. Political B.S., as the Right and Left slammed each other. Shady deals with foreign countries. I assumed only half of the truth was known or printed but it kept people wrongly thinking they were in *The Loop*. A small article was printed at the bottom of page one.

Fake ID's were being printed to get illegal aliens across borders and assume new identities. Most that had been recovered were found to have been linked to a Russian crime syndicate, seeking to hide out in the USA to avoid prosecution. After reading this, I was done with actual news and went to my horoscope.

CHAPTER 5

CAPRICORN HOROSCOPE

Expect the unexpected today. Changes are coming quickly and without reason. Don't question, just adjust. It's really all that can be done about the situations entering your life. Breathe, relax, and let go of being in charge for now.

I made a face. I didn't really trust horoscopes but read mine everyday regardless. I assumed you could apply them to any part of your life if you tried hard enough. But telling a Capricorn to *Let go of being in charge*, made me think my horoscope should have been in the comics.

"What's wrong?" he asked.

"Nothing. Just reading my horoscope," I told him.

"Will you read mine?"

I stared at him for a moment, "Okay. What's your sign?" I asked.

He smirked at the innuendo ridden comment. "Scorpio," he said.

Looking at his drawn-up smirk, I thought, yeah, I could see Scorpio in him.

"Scorpio," I began, "Heads up on all fronts. You may have to go out on a limb to protect the one you love. If there's anything a Scorpio knows it's that in order to do a job well, they may have to bend the rules. You may be out of your comfort zone, but you will always do what needs to be done."

He nodded, more to himself than me.

I put down the paper and started the dialog that I hoped would bring me some answers.

"Ya know," I began, "people will be looking for me...if I don't show up at work."

His face became almost amused at the comment. "Not this week they won't," he said, biting into his cold jammed toast.

"Why don't you think so?" I was worried but didn't want to show it.

"Because...you have the next week off," he told me.

There was no way he could have known this. Even if he did look familiar, I wouldn't have told someone I didn't know, my schedule, or lack thereof. Even at work, they didn't tell people you were on *vacation*. You were just *unavailable*. The only people who knew I was on vacation aside from the people at work were my mom, dad, sister, and best friend an hour away. My heart began to pick up the pace as fear gripped at me all over again.

As if I had willed it, my phone began to ring. "If I don't answer it, she'll worry."

"Who is it?" he got up and looked at the incoming number.

"It's Kris. She calls every Saturday morning," I explained.

"On speaker, no mention of me," he advised, handing me the phone.

I nodded and took my phone from his hand. Answering it, I clicked it to speaker. "Hi Krissy!" something only I could call her. Even her husband didn't get away with calling her this.

"Jesus, were you on the pot? I'd hate to think I made you run, panties around your ankles, for my weekly call."

I had forgotten how we spoke to each other when we thought

no one else was listening. I winced, "No, just doing the dishes, had wet hands."

"Well, that would make sense if you ever used your dishes," she fired back. "Why does it sound like I'm on speaker?"

"Phone is acting up. Sorry. What's up?"

"Are ya coming home for the week or what? Seriously, I've heard every excuse in the book, so shoot, give me a new one."

"I can't," I said staring at my captor.

"No excuse just...no? Are you slipping?" Krissy asked.

"I just have a lot to do here."

"You just don't want to see *HIM*! And because of that, me and the whole family are suffering! Jesus, Gracie, I miss you! I swear I'd come there but I'm kinda in the doghouse with Nate."

Her husband Nathan, Nate for short, was a police Sergeant in the small town we all grew up in. And Kris, well, she was the most likely to cause him angst. "What'd you do now?" I asked.

"I may have...accidentally...egged your Ex's car."

I laughed, "Accidentally? Seriously? We're over and done with. You need to let it go."

The four of us had been best friends for years. But the reasons for the divorce had broken our foursome into a fraction, Three-fourths of the people involved, hated the Ex, Randall. He had actually tried to convince Nate that it was just *the man in him* that made him cheat on me. Nate responded by breaking Randall's nose, then he let Randall know, THAT was from the MAN in him.

"I had let it go," Kris said. "I was doing really well with my anger towards him. Then last night, at the Moose Bar, that jack-ass Ex of yours, got down on one knee and proposed to that skanky mattress accent he cheated on you with and it all just came flooding back."

The air was sucked out of my lungs. He proposed. My face changed. I guess one part of me was upset that his life was moving forward and mine was not. The other part reminded me that he had been moving forward the whole time we had been together.

"I didn't know how to tell you," Kris said to my silence. "I figured egging his car would be a nice *fuck you, you nasty pig* gift, especially since we had freezing temperatures last night. If he uses a snow brush, I think it'll ruin his paint job. Google was a little unsure of the effect. But I figure even if it does no permanent damage, he'll know."

My captor mouthed something to me but I didn't understand. I furrowed my brow and shook my head to indicate that I didn't catch what he was mouthing.

"Are you okay?" he asked out loud.

"Who was that?" Kris asked suspiciously.

I gave him a palms-up. What the hell was I supposed to say now?

"Ugh, hi Krissy," he said.

"Um, no, I am Kris to you...to my husband, to my family. Only Gracie calls me Krissy."

He chuckled, "Very sorry, Kris."

"So ugh, are you the reason she's not in her piece of shit car, headed home right now?"

"Actually, I am," he admitted.

Why was he talking to her? Why would he let her know he was here, especially after telling ME not to tell her? As much confusion as this caused me, it also added some relief, I thought.

"So, what's your name? Or should I just refer to you as the POA?"

"POA?" he repeated.

"Yeah, *Piece of Ass*," she explained.

I closed my eyes and shook my head. The directness that had made us lifelong friends had left her a bit shy in decorum when speaking to others.

He laughed, "My name is Fall Linn."

I shot him a questioning look. Was that really his name?

"As in: Winter, Spring and Summer are your siblings?" Kris asked.

"Well, they would be, if I had any," he added.

"How does one get the name Fall?" she queried.

"My mom moved here from Scotland before I was born. She said that Fall was her favorite season. It reminded her of home. So Fall I am. Plus I was born in the fall."

"So I take it, your name isn't L.Y.N.N.?"

"Nope...Old Gaelic spelling...L.I.N.N."

"So um, no polite way to put this," she started.

I cringed, not knowing what to expect. But knowing it would be personal.

"Shoot," Fall said.

"Have you removed the cobwebs?"

My hands covered my eyes, "Oh my God!"

Fall looked confused for all of five seconds, before he blushed and said, "Uh, no."

Kris never missed a beat, "I know she's a little out of practice, but I'm sure with a little wooing..."

"Okay," I said, taking the conversation back. "That's about enough of that."

"Seriously, it's been well over a year. Your thighs are gonna grow together," Kris told me.

"My thighs are fine," I explained as Fall laughed behind his hand. "Anyway," I changed the subject, "how much trouble are you in for the egging?"

"Oh that. I have to do *The Mechanic*," Kris said with a hint of humor.

I nodded as Fall gave me a confused look. "That's not too bad," I said.

"Nah, it's really not. I actually like having my oil changed, so jokes on him," Kris said. "Anyway, that's on the agenda for tonight," she laughed.

"I do miss you...horribly. I'll try to get home as soon as I can," I told her.

"Maybe you'll come for the wedding?" Kris said sarcastically.

"You're invited to the Ex's wedding?" I questioned.

"Yeah right! I'm gonna crash it," she laughed. "See if I can get Nate to demand *Adam and Eve*."

I shook my head again, "I won't be staying at your house that night," I giggled as Fall's face took on a look of fear and interest.

"Well no duh! We're the only two people in the world!" she answered.

I rolled with laughter then. "I love you."

"I love you, too. Now say goodnight, Gracie."

"Goodnight Gracie," I said and smiled.

"Hey Fall," Kris yelled, "if you kiss her neck right by the collar bone, she'll melt like warm pudding."

"Goodbye Krissy!" I yelled before clicking the *end call* button.

Fall was laughing, "She is something, isn't she?"

"She's an acquired taste," I smiled. "So, why didn't you tell me your name?"

He gave me half a grin, "You never asked."

I nodded. He was right. I hadn't.

"So are you okay? I mean, about your Ex getting married?"

I nodded, "Yeah. I'm actually surprised it took him this long. Some part of me assumed that he would have proposed to her before the ink on the divorce papers dried."

"Even though, it's always hard when the Ex finds someone new," he said.

"Not exactly new," I turned from putting my dish in the sink and faced him. "He cheated on me with her."

Fall winced.

I added, "Our whole marriage," I nodded.

"Damn," he emitted. "That's shitty."

"Yeah, it doesn't exactly do much good for the self esteem," I admitted.

He began shaking his head furiously, "You can't internalize that crap!"

I raised my brows to him, "Really Dr. Phil?"

"No seriously, that's due to his shortcomings...as a breathing functioning human being. It's not a reflection of your worth! Men like him don't care who they hurt. But you can't give him the power to make you accept his lack of respect or conscience, or empathy, as a fault of yours." He was more worked up by this conversation that I had expected, like it had happened to him and not me. Then it dawned on me, maybe I wasn't the only one in this room who has had their heart trampled.

"You sound like you have some first-hand knowledge on the subject," my brow raised.

He swallowed and looked like he was willing himself to calm. "Not really first-hand. Just know that a broken heart...can make some people damage themselves."

"Well, you don't have to worry about that with me. It was never my own neck I pictured in the noose...or hers, for that matter," I added.

"No?" he asked.

"I wasn't married to her and she didn't cheat on me."

The rain had really begun to let loose. The undeveloped, tree covered mountain behind my apartment, was one of my favorite views. It reminded me of home, in a city that didn't. I wasn't sure what I was supposed to or allowed to do now. I finished loading my dishwasher, and wondered if I even had dish soap. I opened the cupboard under the sink and a new bottle was staring at me. Had I had this the whole time, or did he buy it? I never used enough dishes to run the dishwasher.

"So, if you don't mind my asking, what's the mechanic?" Fall asked leaning against the sink. "Kris said she was in trouble with her husband, and she had to DO the mechanic?"

I heard how he heard it.

"Oh," I blushed a bit. "Kris and her husband have kind of a... different way of dealing with their disagreements and fights."

Fall gave a short shake of his head, letting me know he didn't quite understand.

"They have a...*fantasy list* of sorts."

His brow furrowed, still not understanding.

I was trying to explain it without being too explicit. "When one of them is in the doghouse, the other gets to pick out...an act they want their partner to play, to make it up to the other partner."

I watched him roll this around in his mind for a moment. "So...role playing?"

I nodded. "They have a very active sex life."

"Well, that's um...healthy?" he posed it as a question.

"Yeah, I just go with active. They have a three bedroom house and after Kris found out they couldn't have kids, the third room was changed from a nursery to the costume and prop room."

"So one of them plays the mechanic, she doesn't "DO" the mechanic?" he shook his head.

I laughed, "I could hear how this must have sounded to you. No, she just does her husband...in costumes...sometimes with props. I think he's actually the mechanic in this role, not her. But I won't say I'm positive who plays whom, or if they trade off."

"Interesting," Fall said.

It was only ten o'clock in the morning. What the hell was I supposed to do for the rest of the day? "Um, I don't know what to do," I admitted.

"What do you mean?" he asked. "What would you normally do on a day off?"

"I don't know. Watch TV. Read a book. Do my laundry."

"Okay. So why don't you watch TV, or read a book. Or do the laundry," he smiled.

Such a great smile he had, too. I was trying not to be taken in by it, by him. But the fact that he had talked to Kris, had made me less stressed about his *being*. I walked into the living room, not sure what I intended to do. I noticed that he had my fireplace going and the living room blinds twisted open so I could see out, but not the ground. I grabbed one of my many throws and wrapped it around me, before sitting in my normal place on the couch. Clicking on my TV, I sat wondering how to act normal, when normal for me was alone.

"Can I get you anything?" he asked poking his head out of my kitchen.

I knew what I wanted. I wanted to know why he was here. And why was it unsafe for him to leave. I had to get my thoughts straight before I started my questioning. I shook my head no. As he disappeared back into the kitchen, my inner dialog continued. He said it wasn't safe. But did he mean for him or for me? I couldn't imagine how I was in any danger. I knew no one in this town. I mean, I knew my clients, but not on a personal level. I didn't hang out with...anyone. Rarely did I even talk to anyone. Was it possible that he had made a mistake in identity? Maybe he thought I was someone else? But, he called me Grace. He knew my name and I still didn't know why or how. I tried to calm myself with season two of Game of Thrones. I had every season DVR'd so I could watch them all over again from beginning to end. It's amazing how little that does to mellow the nerves: Death, destruction, trusting the wrong people, becoming fodder for mythical creatures due to bad instincts. Crap! When Fall walked out of the kitchen, I jumped.

"Just me," he said displaying his palms in a submissive way. "May I?" he asked pointing to the other end of my couch.

I nodded and he sat. I watched him watching TV.

After a while his facial expressions were hilarious. He winced when someone was brutally killed or put to death. His brows rose as he watched the fight scenes. Then came a naked scene and he looked down, like it was embarrassing to watch. I too felt uncomfortable watching all the flesh on the screen in his presence. I clicked off the TV much to his surprise.

He turned his head so quickly from the screen, his coffee spilled on my carpet. "I'm so sorry," he stood and rushed to the kitchen to grab and wet down paper towels. "That was a little bit...much," he said, turning his deep brown eyes my way.

I laughed at his reaction, "Yeah, little bit," I agreed, "at least to watch with a stranger."

He nodded, "Exactly." Back to the sink he went to wet down more paper towels. "I'm so sorry about your carpet," his head hung.

"It's really not a big deal. I'll get a stain remover recipe from my mother. She knows how to remove any stain from anything."

Fall sat and told me, "Well, if it doesn't work, I'll pay to have them professionally cleaned," he laughed.

After a moment, I said, "I have some questions. I know you can't tell me...everything. But left to my own imagination...I mean, last night, I was scared you were a rapist...or a murderer."

"And today?" he asked, his eyes worried.

"I don't know. I mean, you spoke to Krissy, so some part of me feels...safer. But I don't even know if Fall is your real name. I mean, you could be Psycho Bob, and pretending to be this whole other person."

He stood and pulled out his wallet. Out of its little plastic holder, he handed me a card. It was his license.

He lived in Oregon, in a really nice part on the West side of town. I was right, he was six-four, two hundred and thirty pounds (all muscle I guessed), and was thirty-three years old. I read his name and cocked my head. Fall Linn was the name on the license, "I guess that's really you."

He nodded and took back his license, "I swear, I am exactly who I say I am."

I was a little relieved, but still, I had other questions. "Am I in danger?"

"From me?" he pointed to himself.

I nodded despite the fact that I knew the question may seem offensive.

"No," his eyes showed a deep sincerity. "I would never hurt you, Grace."

"From someone else, then, am I in danger?" fear gripped me again.

He waited then said, "It is a possibility."

My breathing changed. "But...I don't...know anyone! Who would want to hurt me? I mean, I'm just a divorced massage therapist with no social life to speak of."

"That...I can't tell you," he shook his head. "The less you know, the safer you are. But, I'm not going to let anything happen to you."

"Are you a cop?" I asked.

"Something like that," he admitted. "By the way, 'cop' isn't the best term to use. Police Officer is the best way to address them."

"How did you know my name?"

"It's on your mail," he pointed toward the stack on the counter.

I'm not sure if I believed that this was how he knew my name, but it was possible, I guess. "How long are you staying here? How long am I stuck in my house?"

He took a deep breath, "I'm not really sure. I'm hoping to do what I have to do, quickly; but I'm on someone else's time clock at this point. I will tell you this, *this* isn't what I intended. I didn't want to complicate you or your life in any way."

His brown eyes glistened and for some reason I believed him. I still didn't have the heart to tell him that I had no life for him to complicate. I just nodded.

"Can I ask you a question?" he asked.

"I guess so."

"You're pretty tall."

"That's not really a question?" I pointed out.

He smiled, "Why did you buy such a short couch?"

"I don't know. I really like the claw footed look. I couldn't afford the bigger one. Plus, I fit on it. You're just a giant," I smiled.

He nodded and grinned at me.

"I have an air mattress. I sleep on it when mom or Krissy come to visit."

"That would be nice. But I'll sleep on it. No reason for you to be kicked out of your bed," he laughed.

"Yeah, like I was gonna give you my bed," I laughed.

His eyes changed. Biting his lower lip, he quickly turned his gaze to the turned off TV. "So, if not *Games of Thrones*, what else do you like to watch?"

I turned on the TV and went to my DVR so we could find something else to watch. It was then that I realized just how much of a girl I was. Not just a girl, but a hopeless romantic. As I shuffled through my previously recorded movies, I found lots, and lots again, of movies about women who had been jilted, couldn't find love, married some guy in Vegas the first night they met and spent the rest of the movie trying to get away from each other. Women whose lives were made whole by their relationships with their dogs, or cats and so on, until they were sent on a quest for true love. Having someone look at me through my DVR was an embarrassing insight into all that was me. I should have just let him go through my panty drawer, I thought.

"So romantic comedy, huh?" he grinned at me.

Was he making fun of me? Did he put me in that category of

ridiculous women who believe that a fairytale ending still exists? Well, for some, maybe it did. Even if from time to time you had to dress up like a sexy fairy godmother and grant sexual wishes for scratching the car.

"Are you making fun of me?" I asked.

"No actually. *27 Dresses* was a great movie," he gave me a sidelong grin.

"Fine. What would you rather watch? Let me guess, some movie where the guy fights hundreds of men, all at the same time, and kicks the crap out of all of them. But then has to fight the one main bad guy one on one and almost loses. At the last moment he does a totally unexpected roundhouse kick to end the guy who was plotting to take over the world."

"Sarcasm noted. When you put it that way, I guess both kinds of movies seem somewhat ridiculous," he laughed.

"I guess that's what they're for though, entertainment, not realism," I offered.

"So you don't actually believe in happy endings?" he asked.

I raised a brow to him. "I'm a massage therapist. We don't even associate ourselves with the term *happy ending*," I laughed.

"Right, improperly phrased," he nodded. "So, what about love at first sight? Is that a better turn of phrase?"

"Yeah, that's better."

"So...do you? Believe in it, I mean?"

I thought for a moment. "I'd like to." I wouldn't put it out there, but my first glimpse of him, was sure a boot knocker.

"But you don't?" he shook his head.

"Maybe it does happen. But maybe it only happens to a few people. Like their gift."

His brows met, "What do you mean?"

"Well, like some people have musical ability, or are great cooks, or understand math."

He laughed at the last gift listed. "You consider math a gift?"

"Not a gift I was given," I assured him. "But maybe...some people are...love gifted?"

"Hmmm," he mulled this over. "Looooove gifted," he said like a 70's disco disc jockey.

I had to laugh. "Do you believe in it?"

"Yeah. I do." His eyes went misty like he was reliving something in his memory.

I felt a pang of jealousy as I thought of him falling head over heels for some woman and I got my love via movies on my DVR.

"So you don't think there's one person out there for everyone?" he asked.

"God, is that thought disheartening!" I shook my head.

"What do you mean?" he turned his body to face me.

"Well think about it. If there's only one person, I repeat ONE, don't you think the truly broken, love starved, I mean the *truly focused on finding this love* kind of person, would go insane looking for it? There's like seven billion plus people in the world. If there was just ONE, how bleak that would be. What would your chances be of finding that ONE other person who... I guess completes you?"

"Well, you may have single handedly ruined my hope that there's one out there for me."

He's single? I thought. How? "Sorry. Don't mean to be a dream crusher, just a realist. That doesn't always bode well with everyone."

"So you don't believe in true love," he cocked his head.

"Oh, on the contrary," I insisted.

His brows raised again, "Go on."

"I very much believe in true love. I want to find...IT, that, whatever IT is."

"But you haven't found IT?" Fall asked.

"Oh, no!" I shook my head. "I've found laziness, drunkenness, liar-ness, cheater-ness, but not happiness. Although, to be fair, I thought I had once. And for a while, I really was happy. Funny how that changes," I stuck my tongue in my cheek. "You come home early to find your husband doing it doggy-style with your decorator, on your kitchen table!"

He winced, "Yeah, that's pretty bad."

"Yeah, he offered me the table in the divorce."

"Are you kidding?" Fall's eyes rounded.

"Nope, told me that it was well made and sturdy."

Fall shook his head slowly, "Really?"

"Yep, I told him that it did in fact look sturdy from my view, but I was going to take the cookware instead."

"You didn't lose your shit?" he gave me a look of shock. "Sorry about the wording...but really?"

My mind went back to Krissy; standing in our backyard, torching everything Randall owned in our barbeque pit.

"Yeah, I didn't need to," was all I said.

Kris had gotten in a lot of trouble for that one. I mean with her husband. Officially, when my ex-husband tried to accuse her, half the PD swore that she was just trying to extinguish an out of control fire. The fact that she used his entire wardrobe and fishing poles to do so was just the outcome of the panicked thinking of a distraught woman. And even though he tried, Randall could never prove that his four punctured tires and the carving of *Cocksucker* into the hood of his car, was Kris. She had to play *Madame and Sheriff* for that one. Or *Number 21*, as I knew it.

"I don't know how I would have reacted. I mean if I walked in on something like that..." he trailed off, shaking his head.

"Yeah, people said I under-reacted. But I think I may have been in shock. The vision alone was a lot to take in," I nodded. "Then when that wore off, I just felt more humiliated than angry."

"I get that," Fall said. "That would do a number on you. Plus you said that it had gone on..."

"The whole time," I finished his thought.

"I don't mean to sound shocked, but you never had any idea?"

"Well, Randall had a lot of hobbies. He bowled, played baseball with Nate, liked to go fishing and golfing. I just assumed he was busy with the things he enjoyed doing," I gave Fall a sarcastic smile, "I was right. He was doing what he enjoyed. When the marriage ended...literally with a *Bang*," I grinned, "I asked a question I didn't really need to know the answer to...how long? Randall said since twelfth grade. Being a glutton for punishment, I asked why he married me at all, given the fact that he was cheating on me before we even took our vows."

"And?" Fall asked.

"And...Randall said that he loved me...but that didn't stop him from wanting her."

"Ouch."

"Eventually, he fell in love with her...but didn't still want me. So I was voted off *marriage-island* with a view that will forever haunt me."

"Wow," Fall paused and stared off into space. "That's a whole lot of..."

"Fucked up," I added to his pause.

Fall nodded. "And you still believe in love?"

I nodded, "Yeah, I mean look at my parents...or Kris and Nate. Or my sister and her husband." I furrowed my brow. "Maybe I shouldn't include my sister and her husband."

"No?" he asked.

"I haven't heard the man speak in the last two years. He may have gone mute. Or, he may have decided that my sister speaks enough for both of them." Fall laughed, but I let him know, "I'm not kidding. We've had whole conversations, a half hour long, where my only contributions were, 'Really? No! You don't say'. But I mean hey, it works for them, right? They're still together and appear to be happy. So who am I to judge?" I paused. "You know, you've just been listening. How about you? Were you ever married?"

"No. Not even close actually. My job..." he was careful how he answered the question, "I just haven't met the right person, I guess."

In this day and age, the use of the term "Person" instead of woman, made me wonder if maybe he liked his women...to be men. And of course that is perfectly fine (a horrible loss for the females of our specie, but still, fine). "Person," I repeated.

Fall looked confused for about a second, "Woman!" he corrected.

"Was I that transparent?"

"It took me a moment," he nodded laughing. "I date women. Quite a few..."

Jealously! What a weird response to have, I checked myself. But some lucky woman, somewhere, at some point, got to kiss *and then some*, with this guy!

"But, and not to sound like I'm putting all women into a category, but I find that a lot of women like the thought of me, but not really me. I work...a lot. And some women can't handle that. I like my alone time, too...to work on my car or go camping to reset my mind. Take the boat out and go fishing. There are quite a few women who don't enjoy any of those things."

"I don't know if I believe that."

"Well, not the women I've met. I meet most women at the gym..."

"Ah," I said.

"What's 'Ah'?" he asked.

"You just, ya know, look like you spend a lot of time...on your body, that's all."

"Wait, are you calling me a narcissist?" he rounded his eyes at me.

"No...no...no," I said, showing him my palms. "It's just..."

"Just what," he pried on.

"Nothing!"

"You think I only date Barbie's with big fake boobs, nails and eyelashes."

"I didn't say that!" I insisted.

He grinned, "You didn't have to. It was implied," he laughed. "Just so you know...I like women...shaped like women. I like a woman who'll sit down and eat pizza with me, drink beer, and never count a carb or a fat gram."

I laughed.

"I'm not kidding. It gets so old. They bring makeup on camping trips and ask me where they can plug in their straightening iron on my boat. It's a boat for God sakes!" he put his hands to the heavens like he was begging God for the sanity to deal with these women.

"Well, arm candy is still nice, right?" I interjected.

"Not if that's all they are. I mean, a good looking woman should look good without a pint of makeup and hair extensions that fall into my food."

"So we'll go with no, you have not found a true love."

"No. Not yet. But someday I hope," he nodded.

"Yeah, someday," I added, smiling.

We ended up watching ***Goonies***. It was a favorite of mine when I was a kid, and still was. He had never seen the movie and I was afraid it would be a little young for his liking. I was worried he would see the twelve year old braced faced girl in me, emerge from wherever I, and time, had stashed her. But he laughed in all the right places and seemed very amused. At the end of my movie, I let him pick the next, while I made popcorn. He rummaged through my DVD's.

"You don't have a Blu Ray player?" he seemed shocked.

"Um, no," I shook my head. "Is it really that great?"

"It makes the picture so much clearer. That's an investment you should make."

"Okay," I carried two bowls of popcorn with extra butter to the couch. "So, what did you choose?" I asked.

Fall held up a DVD for my approval.

"*Dirty Dancing*?" I laughed.

It was Fall's turn to feign offense. "Hey, this is a great movie. I learned how to dance from this movie."

"You dance?" I laughed.

"Oh, I don't just dance," Fall said, "I can move," he laughed back.

I shook my head trying with all my might not to picture him moving. "Put it on!"

As we sat, each with our own personal popcorn bowls in our laps, Fall asked, "Is there parmesan on this?"

"Yeah. You're not allergic, are you? Or even worse a cheese hater."

He laughed, "No, it's just really good."

"It's how my mom makes it," I said, throwing a handful of popped kernels in my mouth.

I didn't know what was happening but I was having the best time with my captor. As we watched Patrick Swayze pull Jennifer Grey out of the corner, he said, "This is my favorite part. Nobody puts baby in a corner!" he mouthed on cue with the movie. At the end, Fall turned and asked me, "Do you wanna try the lift?"

I looked up at my ceiling fan, "No. I really don't."

Fall laughed, "I can do it, ya know."

"Hold me up? That is quite a feat, but the whole super hero in flight, might not be MY forte. So...what now?" I asked, my ass asleep from sitting for the last four hours.

Just then his pocket began to ring. He looked at the number and said, "I have to take this, your turn to pick a movie." He walked down the hall toward my bedroom before answering.

As I made my way to the chest that housed my movie collection, I could see him out of the corner of my eye. He was whispering, but I did make out a little of his conversation. It went like this:

"It's not what I had planned." Pause. "Well, what if she is?" Pause. "I'm not taking any chances with her!" Pause. "Fine, I'll call you later. Just keep your eyes open and call if anything changes before I get back to you."

I could have made anything out of the conversation. That was the problem. I assumed when he said, "Her" I'm not taking any chances with "Her", he meant me. But I could have been wrong, right? Who was keeping their eyes open? And where was this *watcher* watching from? I was dragged back to reality. I wasn't just having a good time with a great looking guy. I was being kept in my apartment because there may be danger, and it may be directed at me. As he walked back down the hall, his face was drawn again. He was worried, too. And that made my restlessness return to me. I quickly began fumbling through movies and grabbed the first one I could. I held it up for his approval without even looking at the cover.

"Now that's a great movie!" he said.

I turned the case front toward me. *Die Hard.* It was a great movie...not a great life plan.

As I sat back on my half asleep ass, I wondered: if push came to kill, would he be my Bruce Willis? Would he *Yippy-kai-yay* me to safety? I tried to get back to a place of inner calmness. You'd be surprised how hard that is to do when watching *Die Hard* and knowing you may be in the danger-zone.

As the day wore on into late afternoon and my body needed to stretch, my stomach began to growl. Turns out that popcorn couldn't be considered a meal, especially when it ran out four hours ago. I was just about to ask what he'd like to do about dinner, when he said, "We should order a pizza."

CHAPTER 6

FALLING

I wasn't exactly sure how I was going to convince her that I was here for her safety, without exposing why her safety was in question. I couldn't tell her that she was witness to someone who wished to remain un-witnessed. Or that this man had done horrible things to many to keep himself on *ghost status.* She seemed uptight about my presence, and really, who could blame her? She did eat the breakfast I made her. At least she didn't question whether or not I was some psycho who was trying to poison her. I peeked my head out of the kitchen, there she sat, all snuggled in her blanket. She is so beautiful, naturally. Staring at her, she jumped. "Do you need anything?" I blurted out. I want to engage her, but don't want to intrude. Very fine line I was walking.

"May I?" I asked, taking a seat at the far end of her couch. I was so close to her. I hated keeping all of this from her. Omitting seemed more like lying. Some part of me screamed, "For fuck sakes, just tell her!" But I know the extent this man will go to leave no trace of himself. Already, we had found out that the name used on the rental agreement, wasn't his. The BMW he was driving was registered to a company that didn't exist. Only the name on the packages held his true last name. But the first name wasn't on any of his known paperwork or list of previously used personas. His travel visa was in his real name, but we had nothing that we could hold him on. And if we got anything but weren't fast enough, he could choose to use any number of other names and visas to just disappear again.

Grace and I had watched movies for hours when Ernie's number flashed across my phone's screen. Excusing myself down the hall, Ernie let loose.

"What the FUCK?" was the first thing out of his mouth. He wasn't calming down from the predicament I had put us both in.

"She doesn't know anything. Why don't you just wait until she uses the bathroom and get the hell out of there?" Ernie fumed. "She's not in danger, if she doesn't know what the danger is?"

"What if she is?" I asked.

"Do you really think Knushka would *expire* her?"

"I'm not taking any chances with her," I told him.

"FUCK, FUCK, FUCK! This is the craziest thing you've ever done!" Ernie ranted.

CHAPTER 7

KNUSHKA (ALMOST) ON THE HUDSON

Ah the snow. How I miss the snow, Knushka thought to himself. And snow is most beautiful here in my homeland, Russia, than anywhere else in the world. People in Portland Oregon cringe when a few flakes fall…so pampered! We don't raise the weak here, I thought. We do however, raise the stupid, I assessed watching Amsel trying to load the plane. But stupid people were everywhere. As a world traveler, I learned that Darwin should have put on Reaper's uniform, punch timecard and give him a hand. Natural selection was taking too long to weed out the intellectually impaired.

"Should I bring both bottles of vodka?" the tall, thin, dark haired man asked in his thick Russian accent.

"What else we do with them?" I asked.

Amsel looked as though his mind went blank with the possibilities of responses that could be right.

"Yes, yes, yes," I rubbed my temple, wondering how he managed to remember to breathe.

Truth be told, he is my nephew, or I would have made his head into a drive-thru, many years ago. My dear sister, Anna, who had practically raised me, was his mother. She taught me how to shoot at the ripe age of eight. She instructed my very first Columbian Neck Tie at the age of twelve, even though I made quite a mess. She showed only love and patience for the small boy whose hands were not yet strong. She was a Saint. And for all her saintly duties, all of her teaching and instructing, she had been gifted a bowl of pudding with legs for a son. But she loved him well.

Up the steps of my small jet, Amsel lumbered. A bottle in each hand, he bounced his head off of the sign that clearly read in Russian, **CAUTION! Low Doorway**. I stood there shaking my own head wondering if my dear sister would truly miss this gene puddle, should he meet with an accident at two thousand feet (like suffocating from bag over head twisted closed at neck).

My own son, Dmitri Jr., was being kept busy by the birth of his fourth child, or I would have been using his expertise on this trip, instead of pudding boy.

After the plane was packed and all the fabricated documents necessary to enter the US were accounted for, we would head to the hospital so I could see my new grandson. A real chip off the old block, I'm sure. My son and grandsons were handsome, smart and not afraid to get their hands dirty, literally.

I blame Amsel's stupidity on his father's contribution to his procreation.

I was not brokenhearted when my sister, severely disgraced by her husband, asked that I dole out his sentence. To honor her, I repeated the neck tie she had taught me so many years ago. Never again would he insult her borscht. I smiled to myself at the memory of him gurgling and flailing as the life oozed out of him.

I waited in the backseat of the Rolls for Amsel to disembark the plane. At which time, he knocked himself backward into the plane on the same caution sign. I let out a heavy sigh and shook my head again. Amsel would test the patience of a monk. And monk, I was not. A moment or two later, I saw him sit up and shake his head. Shoulder length hair whipping around, like a puppy that has had his bell rung. But as I am perfectly aware, he has no bell to ring.

CHAPTER 8

A LITTLE LESS COVERSATION, A LITTLE MORE ACTION

"So, can I go take a shower?" I asked.

"I don't know, can you?" Fall replied.

"If you're waiting for me to ask 'may I', I'm going to start to smell really bad."

Fall laughed, "Of course you can. You can do everything you usually do."

"Except leave the house," I reiterated.

"Except that," he nodded his head.

I went into my room to grab some jammies. After all, having a house guest (of sorts), meant I wouldn't be walking around naked. Not that I did that very much. But I was known to walk from the shower to my room, bare assed, from time to time.

Opening my jammie drawer, I couldn't help but wonder if I should wear something a little more...well, not sexy. But not frumpy, I thought, Holding up my grey men's sweat pants, I thought, they might be a little too *I really don't care what I look like*, in a bad way. It was okay not to care what I looked like with no one else here. But these sweats didn't say, *I'm confident in who I am and I choose to be comfortable.* They said *I'm one week away from buying a house full of cats and eating pork and beans right out of a can*. I wanted just a little less, *I've given up*, than that. I grabbed my pink sweats and a baby T. Comfortable, yes, but not *I'm going to scrub the gunk off the shower tiles'*, comfortable.

As I lay in the tub, I looked down at my body. What was I thinking? He dated gym girls. Even though I exercised daily, I didn't pump iron, or spend hours high kicking or doing Pilates. Not only that, this guy wasn't a potential...anything. He was some guy who had convinced me he wasn't totally crazy and was here to protect me from things he couldn't explain to me. When I put it that way, I looked at the door lock. It was engaged and that gave me a little false security. I mean seriously, he knew how to pick a lock. That I already knew. Then again, I had spent the whole day with him and he was a perfect gentleman. More than that really, he was THE perfect gentleman. Handsome, smart, witty, great sense of humor, and could cook perfect eggs (which to me seemed to be harder than making a good roast). I checked my legs to see if I was a stubble farm then shaved.

Out of the bath, I did the lotion thing and brushed my hair. I couldn't stand the thought of being braless in front of him. It seemed indecent, not to mention uncomfortable. So back in the boob sling they went.

There was a knock at the door, "Ya almost done in there?" Fall asked.

"You're not gonna ask if I started again, because not much has changed in the last eight hours."

"No," he laughed.

"Good," I grinned at the door.

"I ordered pizza and it will be here in a few minutes. Is that okay?"

"Sure. I'll be right out." I had secretly been craving pizza for a few days. And it was even the plan for last night before my world went wacky.

I put my clothes in the washer and headed back to the living room. But there was no Fall. A small glow from the kitchen called my attention. There on my table/island, sat two plates, two glasses of red wine, and a candle flickering. Fall appeared from behind me, making me look around. Where the hell had he come from? He hadn't been in my living room or kitchen. But I saw he was wearing sweat pants, too.

"You changed your clothes?" It was a question and an observation.

"Yeah, I needed to get out of those jeans, especially if I'm going to eat pizza," he patted his nonexistent stomach.

"You have clothes here? How?" I questioned.

"Oh I had Ernie drop off my bag. I hope you don't mind," he shook his head.

I couldn't seem to put the words into words. My thoughts ran as I tried to decide which question to ask first. "Who's Ernie?" came out first.

Fall looked apprehensive, "He's my..."

As he figured out what word to use as well, my mind rolled forward. Gardener, barber, imaginary friend...

"He's my...partner." His eyes held a tinge of "I want to tell you," but his body language said, "Please don't ask anymore."

"And he was here...while I was in the bath?"

"Yeah, he's not a big errand runner, so he grumbled at bit first. But in the end, I can always count on him," he said looking down at his sweats and fresh shirt.

"So...um...how long are you staying?" I was trying not to sound like I wanted him gone, because I wasn't sure I did. But I wasn't used to...men anymore. Was he going to leave beard hair in my sink? Leave his towel on my floor? Leave a floater in my toilet? That last one was a rare marriage moment for me, but the scar it left, ran deep.

His mouth stretched into a wince, "I'm hoping...not too much longer. I hate infringing on you..."

"No, no, not at all," It sounded somewhat forced, I'm sure. I just didn't know what to make of all this. I was only in the bathroom for half an hour, which would have been less if I hadn't shaved my wholly mammoth legs. Ernie must have been close by. So close in fact, I didn't understand why Fall was staying with me. Was the danger that close?

CHAPTER 9

BABIES AND BRAKELINES

"Would you like to hold your grandson, Papa?" Dmitri Jr. asked his father.

"Bring him to me, my little prince," Knushka said, holding out his arms.

The other three grandsons, ages three, five and seven, ran around the room like little mad men. His daughter-in-law, a birthing champ, looked like she had been admitted for a hangnail.

"You are well, Elana?" Knushka asked her.

"I am well, father. I delivered this one even before the doctor arrived."

"Why was he not here to birth my grandson?" Knushka's Russian accent thickening with agitation, his jaw tightened.

"He stopped to see another woman in labor and missed the birth," his son told him. "She delivered so quickly," Dmitri Jr. said, kissing his wife's brow.

"I see," Knushka said. "But child is well?" he asked looking into the face of grandson number four.

"He's fine, Papa," Elana said. "He's perfect."

"Good, good," is what he said. But, mentally Knushka was already having the doctor taken care of.

As Knushka walked to the Rolls with Amsel at his side, he gave him clear instructions. "I want the doctor's brake line cut."

"But how I know which car is his?" Amsel wanted to know.

"I bought him the car after my third grandson was born. It has personal plate. *DOC 1*."

"I will do this!" Amsel said, nodding his head.

There they sat in silence, Knushka staring at the back of Amsel's head. "Well what are you waiting for?"

"Oh, you wanted I do this now?" Amsel asked, surprised.

Knushka took a few deep breaths through his nose before answering, "Yes. I want you do this now."

"I wasn't sure. I mean, could have done it when we get back from US, or could have waited for birthday, or could have..."

"For. The. Love. Of. All. That. Is. Holy. DO IT NOW!" Knushka flared. "Take water jug with you!"

As Amsel exited the Rolls, Knushka began to mumble under his breath. "Stupid. Could not have come from our lineage! Oatmeal! Oatmeal thinks more than he does!"

A few minutes later as the Rolls rolled past the doctors Mercedes, Knushka asked, "Why is brake fluid on the ground?"

"I cut line," Amsel pointed to the large puddle beginning to ooze.

"What did you do with water jug?" Knushka's face squished up.

Amsel thought, "I make pee," he said lifting the jug half-full of urine.

Knushka was back to deep nose breathing, "The jug was so no trace of brake fluid would be seen and doctor would not suspect danger until brakes no work."

"I put snow over puddle?" Amsel asked as a solution.

"Drive!" Knushka said defeated.

Knushka rode silently, his rage simmering as he rubbed his temple. He lived by rules of murder, the first: Should Divine

Intervention be made, he would see it as God's will and never raise a hand to the intended victim again. He wasn't sure *stupidity of his Hitter*, was considered Divine. But this was the rule.

He pondered whether or not God would interfere should he *piano wire* Amsel. The rest of the drive, he imagined murdering his nephew in numerous ways. Before he knew it, he was smiling again.

CHAPTER 10

BACK IN THE GOOD OL' USA

"What's your name, sugar?" he asked. Her pouty red lips, full and plump, would work nicely he thought.

"Janine," she said, batting her long black lashes.

"Well Janine, you need a new battery or you won't be getting very far," he said looking under the hood of her car.

"Oh no! How much will that cost?" she pretended to look under the hood as well, bending at the hips. Janine in her pin-up red polka-dot dress gave him quite an eye-full, as her assets were well displayed.

"At least $100, if I don't find anything else wrong," he grinned.

Janine looked at the nametag on his overalls, "Bob is it?" she asked him.

Bob nodded.

"I don't have that kind of money," she licked her lips. "I'm trying to get out to Hollywood and I barely have enough money for gas as it is," Janine bit her bottom lip. "I'm desperate," she explained. "Is there any way you could help a girl out?" she reached out tentatively to rub his already swollen bulge.

Bob smiled and began unzipping, "I think we may be able to help each other out."

Janine dropped to her knees then looked up at him, "I think I need an oil change, too."

Bob grinned down at her, "This may mess up your lipstick, sweetheart."

After the fun, Krissy and Nate lay in each other's arms, both spent. Krissy asked her husband, "Should I use a different name next time? Janine didn't quite feel like...right! Ya know? Wanda maybe?" she threw the name out for his approval.

"Baby, you can use whatever name you want, as long as you bring those lips to this party," he kissed her hard and deep.

The *Mechanic*, or #16, had left them both very pleased.

CHAPTER 11

FALLING

The doorbell rang and I had Grace answer the door. After all, this was her regular Pizza place and I didn't want them to know she had company. I could hear the whole conversation from the hallway.

"Wow, you don't ever order a large," said her delivery boy.

I stole a glance of him. Early 20's, long blonde hair on top, shaved on the back and sides. He looked like the kind of guy who spent hours in his basement apartment at his parent's house, stoned and playing video games.

"Yeah, I know," Gracie said, taking the giant pie box.

The delivery boy looked passed her, "You, uh, got company?"

"No, no," Gracie said, "just love the leftovers."

"Well, if you ever want company..."

My eyes flashed. Really? This little doofus was hitting on her?

"I could drop by. I'm off at 11:00," said the pizza pusher.

"That's sweet, but I'll be in bed by then," Gracie said.

"Lucky bed," the delivery boy countered, grinning like an idiot.

Grace smiled, handed him his tip and said goodnight.

As Grace walked back into the kitchen, I said, "Even the pizza boy hits on you," and laughed.

"Yeah, he's actually the only one who hits on me," she said.

"I find that hard to believe. Your customers don't hit on you?" I asked.

"Clients, not customers and no, we aren't allowed to date our clients," she grinned.

God, I loved that smile. "But they could still hit on you," I pointed out.

"No, it's kind of our thing, if they do hit on you, you pass them off to another L.M.T. It's our policy," she added, grabbing the plates off the table and serving up slices for her and myself.

"So you've never been hit-on at your job," I asked. "I find that hard to believe."

We took our plates to the little table/island, "Maybe once. But I wasn't sure," she crinkled up her nose.

"You weren't sure?" my eyebrows raised.

"Well, he asked for my home phone number," she took a bite of her pizza.

"That didn't seem like a come-on to you?" I laughed.

"Not really. A lot of people want in-home massage. But we don't offer that, so I just told him it was against policy and he never asked again."

I nodded pretty sure she was being naive. It was obvious though that she had no idea how beautiful she was and was kind enough to always think the best of people. Pretty amazing given what her Ex had put her through.

"This is my favorite pizza," she said, eyeing me closely.

I grinned, "Mine too."

"When did you get the wine?" she wanted to know.

"This morning, when I bought stuff to make breakfast," I said blankly.

She was still staring at me, “So you knew you’d be here for dinner?”

“I assumed,” I nodded and took a bite.

“But you don’t know how long you’ll be here?”

I loved watching her lips move and if I wasn’t careful, it was going to creep her out, the way I kept staring at them. I deliberately dropped my eyes. “I really don’t,” I admitted. “I’m really sorry if my being here has been an inconvenience and I do wish I could tell you more, but...”

She nodded before I could finish my thought, “I know...you’re protecting me.”

Her eyes seemed different all of the sudden, like she saw ME differently. With everything I had, I wanted to grab her, touch her, kiss her. That *look* left me hungrier than ever for her. That *look* said she trusted me.

CHAPTER 12

PIZZA FOR TWO

Usually the delivery boy didn't put me on edge, but tonight felt different as Fall hid in my hallway. We did our normal banter; him asking if I wanted company and, as always, I smiled and said "no thank you". I had gotten used to this from my friendly neighborhood pizza boy and wrote it off as a joke.

As I plated some slices for Fall and me, I noted that this was the exact same pizza I ordered every time; Pepperoni, jalapeno, and pineapple. It seemed like a far-fetched favorite to be both of ours, but I didn't want to seem too concerned that I had possibly been stalked by him. What a horrible thing to think of him, I told myself. The wine made me wonder if he was just being polite for his intrusion of my life, or was this...something else? He asked a few questions about being hit-on, which made me laugh. If he only knew how little anyone paid attention to me, and how little I did to get attention, he would have found it laughable, too.

"Truth is," I said, "I don't date. My only links to the outside world are work, my family and Krissy. I guess that's why I'm having so much trouble figuring out how I can be in danger."

Fall quickly changed the subject. "That Krissy seems like a firecracker. Her husband must have a great sense of humor," Fall said between bites.

"Nate really does. You wouldn't expect that from a cop. I mean police officer," I corrected myself for his benefit.

"Nate's an officer?" Fall lifted his brows.

"Yep, his whole family," I nodded and took another bite.

"How long have you known him?" Fall asked.

"Oh, we've all known each other since grade school," I said.

"Really?" Fall nodded. "So, were he and Kris always an item?"

"No, they were always friends, but Krissy thought that Nate was too much of a goody-goody and was destined to follow his family's shoes and become an officer. She didn't want to date an officer," I smiled. "I believe she had bad-boy-syndrome for a while there."

"So what changed?" Fall asked.

"Ah," I grinned. "One night, out at the place down by the lake where all the cool high school kids hung out," I made air quotes, "Krissy brought a date to the bonfire. He was a little older, went to the university. Very handsome," I added.

"Oh yeah," Fall grinned. "So what was wrong with Mr. Handsome?"

"Mr. Handsome," I grinned, "wouldn't take *NO* for an answer."

The look on Fall's face became grim, as he nodded in understanding.

"Anyway, Mr. Handsome had asked Krissy to take a walk in the woods with him. None of us thought anything of it. I mean there were like fifty people there," I explained. "Then we heard it...Krissy let out a scream, and that was all it took. Nate went running into the forest and found Krissy coming down the path with a torn shirt and bra-strap. She had a slap mark just staring to redden on her cheek."

Fall listened intently, as I continued.

"Well, Nate took one look at her and ran off into the woods. Krissy was screaming for him to come back. I guess Mr. Handsome was on the wrestling team and was known to be quite an ass beater. Not to mention the fact that the guy had forty pounds and four inches on Nate," I raised my brows. "Krissy ran after Nate to save his ass from an imminent beating. She said she followed the sounds of someone taking a good licking. She was so worried for Nate," I added. "When she found them, Mr. Handsome was on the ground, bleeding from his broken nose."

Fall's smile stretched across his face.

"When Krissy ran up, Nate was yelling at Mr. Handsome, "That girl," he pointed to her, "That girl right there, that's my girl! You ever touch her again...a broken nose will be the least of your problems'," he told him."

"Damn," Fall said, nodding his respect. "Then what happened?"

"Nate walked right up to her, all sweaty and out of breath and laid a lip lock on her that she swears curled her damn toes," I laughed. "She jumped up in his arms, wrapped her legs around him, and she's been wrapping her legs around only him ever since," I laughed.

"So he always knew?" Fall said.

"Nate swears that from the first moment they met, in pre-school," I added, "he knew she was the one."

"That's pretty cool," Fall said. "So your ex-husband knows Nate."

I nodded, "Oh yeah. Randall was Nate's best friend all the way through school. He and I started dating after Krissy and Nate got together."

"So...Krissy has done some stuff to your Ex, is what I gathered from the whole *egging* admission."

I let out a deep breath, "Off the record?" I asked.

"Completely," Fall agreed.

"Yeah, she's done some stuff," I nodded.

"Like what?" Fall's grin was mischievous.

"Well," I still wasn't sure how much I wanted to tell him.

"I promise, I won't tell anyone," Fall held up a *scouts honor* sign.

"We're you a scout?" I asked.

He laughed, "No, I wasn't," he shook his head.

I gave him a sidelong look, "Are you willing to *pinky swear*?" I smiled.

CHAPTER 13

COMEDY AND TRAGEDY

Knushka boarded the jet that would take him from Russia to New York. At least on this trip, he had no fear of going through customs, as everything had been shipped ahead of time. His *buyer* in New York was an old friend and if ever he trusted anyone, at all, it was this man they called Slovak.

Taking his seat, all he wanted was a double-vodka on the rocks and some quiet. Once his first gulp went down, he sighed and let his head fall back into pure relaxation.

"*Bong-ding-bong, bong-ding-bong,*" went Amsel's game on his phone. Again and again, it rang out, "*Bong-ding-bong.*" Every nerve in Knushka's body was being put on edge. His left eye began to twitch furiously, as the sound bore into his brain.

Finally, he lost it, "Please, you turn off that infernal racket!" he yelled.

"I turn off sound, I know not what happens in game," Amsel said.

Mentally, Knushka was counting to ten and trying to banish visions of beating Amsel to death with his phone.

"I don't care what happens in game," Knushka said through a tightened jaw. "I'm not flying across ocean listening to this Bong-ding-dong racket." He could feel his blood pressure rising, "You have choices to make. Either turn off sound...or try to retrieve phone from rectum," Knushka's stone-cold gray eyes were fixed.

Amsel looked like a hound that had been kicked, "I turn off sound," he said into his chest.

Knushka went back to his vodka as the pilot gave them their cruising speed and altitude from a speaker overhead. It was going to be a long trip that he hoped to sleep through.

CHAPTER 14

KRISSY...UNLEASHED

I was laughing my ass off, "So Kris just put the fish in his heating vent?" I asked Grace.

"Oh no," she said, trying to stop laughing long enough to speak, "she cut it up...into tiny little pieces...then put it in EVERY vent in the house. Took him forever AND professional help, to remove the damned thing."

I shook my head, "My God, don't ever let me piss this woman off."

"Don't ever mess with me, then you won't ever have to worry about it," Gracie laughed.

"And the suds," I shook my head, "Genius!"

"Yep, she would've gotten trespassing and vandalism for that one if Randall's neighbors didn't hate him so damn much," she giggled. "They swore they never saw her; even though that was that day the wife gave Kris her pot roast recipe."

"You have to admit though, dish soap in the Jacuzzi was one thing, but in the dishwasher and washing machine, too! I bow my head to her," I nodded.

"Suds with green dye through the whole house...ruined their carpet," Gracie added.

I stood and grabbed another bottle of wine, "What do ya think...should we open it?" I asked her.

She made a face like she was weighing what to do then finally smiled, "Well, I ***am*** on vacation."

I smiled back, "Yes you are. It might not be what you planned..."

She cut me off, "Actually, this is the most fun I've had in a long time."

Her smile, this moment...was almost enough to send all of my worries running. I had to admit, as much of a fuck-up as I had made breaking into her house, I wouldn't trade this night for anything. I opened the second bottle and poured her a glass.

"So has Kris always been like this?" I needed to know.

"She's always been outspoken...direct, but her vandalizing only started after everyone and their mother, and mine by the way," she grinned, "found out about what Randall had done to me...or was doing to someone else," she smiled that smile that I had already fallen for. "Since we had all been so close, Krissy felt like he had cheated on all of us."

I nodded, "Makes sense to me. I'd love to meet the person who has your back to the point of possible jail time."

She just smiled. I wasn't sure how to read her. Was this a *that would be nice* grin, or a *you're not going to be in my life that long* grin. "I'm sure she already knows all about you," Grace finally said.

"Why do you say that?" I laughed.

"Please...she *HAS* your name! She's probably already asked Nate to run a complete background check on you. By tomorrow, she'll know everything from what size pants you wear to whether or not you've ever dowloaded porn."

I nodded, "Oh is that how it is?" I laughed.

She shrugged her shoulders, "What can I say...I'm family to her. Not to mention she has the inside track on everyone and their secrets."

I tried not to look worried. "Do you mind if I put on some music?" I asked.

CHAPTER 15

GRACEFUL, BE DAMNED

Fall opened a second bottle of wine and poured me a glass. I was starting to feel very warm. But to be honest, he drank more than me.

"Do you mind if I put on some music?" he asked.

I nodded to him, "Sure." I was curious to see what his taste in music would be. Would he go for hard rock, classic, gospel? I mean, I couldn't rule anything out with what little I knew about him. His music choice might give me some insight into who he was, or what he's like.

I watched him bending over my stereo. I didn't splurge on much (that was just the truth), but my stereo? That may have been the only thing I owned worth stealing. He had such a great backside," I cocked my head, enjoying the view. I heard my CD changer open, and wondered which one, from literally hundreds, he had chosen? From the very first note, my eyes fell closed and I smiled from ear to ear as goose bumps took over my flesh: *These Arms of Mine*, by the brilliant Mr. Otis Redding, rang out. Not just one of the most well-sung songs in my opinion, but one of the sexiest, too. As Fall walked back over to me, I opened my eyes.

"You have some great music," he said, giving me the grin I was becoming very fond of.

"And you, apparently, have excellent taste in music," I raised my wine glass to him.

"Oh, I love Otis. My mother always played Otis Redding to unwind after a hard day of work," Fall took his seat.

"You're close to your mom?" I asked.

"We don't get to see each other as much as I'd like. She lives in New York," he explained. "But we talk on the phone about once a week, or so. She's a wonderful woman, actually amazing," he added. "I couldn't have asked for a better mother."

Hearing this made me smile. I was raised to believe that any man, who openly loved and appreciated his mother, was a gem.

"So were you raised in New York?"

"No, I was raised here in the Great Northwest. She moved to New York for her job," he nodded.

"What does she do?" I asked.

Fall's face took on a moment of contemplation, "She's an agent," he said matter-of-factly, then took a sip of his wine.

I got the feeling he wasn't going to elaborate, but why? Was she a travel agent, literary agent, real estate agent?

"Would you like to dance?" Fall's eyes met mine.

I wanted to, more than just about anything, but all of the sudden this just seemed so surreal. What was happening here? What role did he play in my life? Why was I having the best night I could remember in years...with a perfect stranger? Not to mention, one who had basically taken me hostage, for lack of another explanation. He watched as I mulled these thoughts over.

"I'm sorry. That must have seemed at the very least awkward, if not inappropriate," he began, "I didn't mean to make this more uncomfortable than this must already be for you," he shook his head.

I couldn't help but smile, "Yes," I said.

"That's what I was afraid of..."

He misunderstood the comment. I cut him off, "No. I mean, *yes*, I'd like to dance."

"Oh," his face showed both surprise and relief as he offered me his hand.

We stood and moved to my small living room. Otis Redding's *I've Been Loving You Too Long* began to play as he took one of my hands in his and put the other on my hip.

CHAPTER 16

FALLING HARDER

It took every bit of my guts to ask her to dance. The look on her face made my brain scream *abort*. I had just crossed a line that would make this situation weirder than it already was. I began stammering apologies. *Dammit*, my brain yelled at me. Why did I have to...she cut my thoughts of regret short.

"I'd like to dance," she smiled at me.

It was like my heart began to pound again. In fact, it was like it was threatening to beat clean out of my chest, as I took her hand and led her to the living room. I didn't want to scare her, didn't want to seem too imposing. I took her hand in mine then placed the other hand on her hip.

I kept room between us, although every part of me wanted to feel what her body would feel like against mine. As we swayed I was aware of everything about her: Her scent; vanilla. Her hand; warm. She was soft to the touch; welcoming. I could feel the curve of her hip as it swayed back and forth. I tried not to think of how badly I wanted to caress them, pull her against me by them. I knew that once this song ended, I would miss touching her this way. For just a moment she looked up into my eyes and my overbeating heart raced even faster. I was afraid what my eyes might give away but I couldn't help looking longingly at her mouth, I wanted her kiss so badly...wanted her lips against mine, to feel the warmth of her mouth, taste the sweetness. She looked down. I thought I had lost her, scared her, but then she moved closer. Wrapping her arms around my neck, her head laid against my chest. We were now body to body, and just like I had known it would, her body felt so right against mine. As the song ended I stopped swaying. The thought of moving away from her caused an aching. Then *You're Still My Baby* started and she looked up, bit her lower lip and asked, "One more?" I smiled as I moved my body back against hers.

CHAPTER 17

GRACEFULLY

As he led me to the living room my heart began to pound. He was so tentative, like I was a porcelain doll, as he took my hand in his. His other hand found the curve of my hip. I hadn't been touched in so long that the feeling, the warmth of his hand through my clothes, almost made my knees weak. But it wasn't just the touch of anyone who would have done this to me. It was *him*, and I knew it. I could smell his faded cologne. It was intoxicating and made my mouth water. Every inch of me wanted to be closer to him, wanted to feel his arms around me, wanted to feel his body against mine. I looked up and met his stare. It was there...I saw it. The way he looked at me made a blush rise to my cheeks. His mouth, I wanted it. I had to look away for fear that my eyes would scream my yearning for him. I took a step into his body and wrapped my arms around his neck and laid my cheek against his chest, listening to his heart beating as madly as my own. I felt his body relax as though he had been waiting to do the very same thing. His arms wrapped around me...held me close. I was trying not to get lost in this moment the closest thing to pure ecstasy I had felt in years. As the song began to fade he pulled away just a little, but I didn't want this to end. "One more?" I asked, biting my lower lip to keep from kissing him. He drew me back against him and I was almost to heaven.

CHAPTER 18

FALLING GRACEFULLY

I had no Idea how this night was going to end...and didn't care. I was holding the woman I had been falling for, for the past three months. She was in my arms, real, warm and soft. I tried to keep the visions at bay. But I couldn't stop seeing me kissing her mouth, her neck. Suddenly I realized that the thoughts I had let run away were manifesting in a very physical way. As long as she was in my arms the visions were sure to come. And as long as the visions came this would be a problem. I had never had this strong of a reaction to any other woman. Well, at least not since ninth grade. I couldn't calm him down. I knew I wasn't a hormonal teenager anymore, but I had to move away from her so I wouldn't offend her and embarrass myself. I took a step back and said, "More wine?"

CHAPTER 19

HUH???

I was in my own world. As we swayed, I pictured kissing his mouth, over and over again. Kisses that started out so sweet, gentle and telling. His neck was right there, and every part of me was fighting not to press my lips to it. More thoughts were emerging as I saw the passion building in my mind's eye.

"More wine?" Fall suddenly asked, moving his body away from mine.

What had I done? What was wrong? "Ugh, yeah," was all I could say as we headed back into the kitchen. He seemed different now. He was avoiding my eyes. As he turned his back to grab the wine, I did a breath check. No, that wasn't it. Plus he ate the same pizza and drank the same wine as me. I didn't have time to do a pit-check before he turned back around, but I had taken a shower and used deodorant. What could it have been? Then it hit me, maybe I misinterpreted *the look*. Oh, how humiliating! I was sure he caught the look I gave him. So he must have been freaked by it and had to find an excuse to get away from me before I threw myself at him. I was so embarrassed; I just wanted to find a hole to climb in.

CHAPTER 20

FALLING DOWN

Oh God, she was looking at me differently. She knew, had to know. I had my chance with her and I blew it. I grabbed the wine and tried to paint on a *I'm not a pervert* smile. To be honest, I wasn't even sure what one of those looked like. Then she confirmed my suspicions.

"It's getting late. I should probably get the blow-up mattress and let you get some sleep," she said.

"Yeah, that would be great, thank you." Not how I wanted this night to end. I would have been content to just hold her and dance if it weren't for the awkwardness that would arise when a part of me stood at attention.

We set up the mattress and she grabbed her extra blankets, then she said, "Is there anything else you need before I go to bed?"

"If it's okay, I think I need to use your shower," I answered.

"Of course. The towels are in there," she pointed to the hall closet. "I'm sorry I don't have any more manly body wash, just the vanilla that's in there."

"It's okay. Ernie brought mine."

"Oh, good, well, goodnight," she said, heading to her room and closing the door behind her.

I let out a deep breath and said under my breath, “A cold shower. Very...very...cold!”

CHAPTER 21

GRACELESS

Lying in the dark and staring up at the ceiling, it was blacker than pitch, but I couldn't close my eyes. I was beyond embarrassed. I heard the shower turn on and couldn't help but wonder if Fall was trying to wash *me* off of him. How could I have gotten it so wrong? I was so sure he felt...well, something for me. So I guess he asked me to dance because he likes dancing, not me. He had actually already said as much when we watched *Dirty Dancing*. I put my hands over my eyes to block my thoughts not the absence of light.

CHAPTER 22

FALLING DOWN AGAIN

I jumped in the shower and almost let out a yelp from the cold. Normally I would handle this kind of frustration a different way. But this wasn't just frustration I was feeling. I was humiliated, seeing her face over and over again as she avoided my eyes. It was going so well. I looked down at my manhood shrinking against the cold and told him, "It serves you right. What were you thinking?" Then I remembered what I was thinking. I tried to push the images out of my head so we wouldn't have a repeat of what started this whole mess in the first place. It was nice though, I thought. The smell of her, the feeling of her body against mine..."Are ya kidding me?" I said looking down.

I finished showering as quickly as I could and got under the covers determined to fall asleep as quickly as possible. An hour later I was laying in the dark staring at her closed bedroom door. Part of me thought I should have taken care of this issue in the shower. The other part of me didn't think it would have helped.

CHAPTER 23

CHECKING IN, OR CHECKING OUT

New York was no slouch when it came to snow. As the plane landed, all was covered in a blanket of white. Off the jet, Knushka walked to his waiting limo. From the warmth of the backseat he could see Amsel trying to carry all of the luggage in one trip. A smile emerged as Amsel tumbled down the stairs. He wondered if a knock to the brain would help. He had already decided it could not hinder his nephew.

Pulling up in front of the hotel, Amsel started loading the bags onto a cart.

"Not that one," Knushka said, pointing to a small black case. "That one, you carry!"

"But I don't have to carry, that is what cart is for," Amsel retorted.

Again he felt his blood pressure rising. "I said," he leaned in to make himself as clear as possible, "YOU CARRY!"

At the front desk he said to the man manning the post, "Cocovo, reservation for two rooms."

"Oh, we only hold rooms till 8pm. I'm afraid we gave one of your rooms away two hours ago. We still have the one room available, though," smiled the desk puppet.

"One room?" Knushka said, looking over his shoulder at Amsel, who was cleaning his ear with his fingernail and then inspecting what he removed.

After a long, disgusted pause, Knushka let out a long sigh and said, "Fine."

As the elevator door closed, "What floor for you sir?" asked the thin blonde man with his *customer service* smile painted on thick.

"Twelve please," Knushka answered.

Amsel was back to playing the game on his phone. Knushka looked down to see the small case had been put on the floor at Amsel's feet.

Quietly, Knushka told Amsel, "Put phone away and pick up case."

Amsel reached down and picked up the case, but continued to play his game.

Knushka noted how Amsel was distorting his hands to keep playing and said again, "Put phone away!"

"I can do both," Amsel began to argue, showing Knushka that it wasn't that hard. That's when it happened; Amsel fumbled, his phone flying up in the air. To save his phone he dropped the hard case to the ground. To the floor it fell, springing open. Out tumbled a Glock 40 cal. and two ammo clips. The elevator operator's eyes went to it and widened with fear. His hand reached for the emergency button; but before he could press it, Knushka knocked him out cold with a right hook.

Looking both ways down the hall, Knushka pushed his trolley cart towards his room. He had Amsel place the body of the elevator operator on top of his luggage then put his trench coat over him to block the body from the cameras. Amsel, who walked behind Knushka, was sporting what would eventually become a black eye.

In the room, Knushka ordered Amsel to go get ice.

Amsel grabbed the small ice cup provided that sat next to the coffee maker and headed for the door.

"What are you doing?" Knushka asked him, his face red with anger.

Amsel held up the ice cup, "I get ice. Like you asked."

Knushka was back to counting again, "1...2...3..."

"Why you counting?" Amsel looked more confused than normal.

Knushka put a finger up to silence his nephew, "1...2...3..." he started over. When he hit 10, he said, "Empty suitcase, take suitcase to ice machine, fill it with ice, and bring back to room. You understand?"

The look on Amsel's face showed that he didn't understand, but he did what he was told, anyway.

CHAPTER 24

THE MORNING COMETH

I answered the phone on the second ring. I didn't want it to wake Gracie, even though I knew she was an early riser. Actually, I was afraid to see Gracie. It was Ernie with news.

"Hey stud," Ernie said.

"Very Funny," I told him, walking to the coffee maker.

"How did last night go? Any *living vicariously* I should be doing?"

"No," I told him. "Just moments of utter humiliation, did you want to share in that?"

"Maybe. The thought of a woman humiliating you, makes me think she's not just taken in by looks, money, body..."

"Yeah, yeah," Fall said, filling the coffee maker with water. "What do you have for me?"

"Our man has landed. He flew into a private airstrip in New York then checked into The Park Plaza. We have eyes on him. He'll probably be back here by tomorrow or the day after."

"Great," I told him.

"So yeah, now that you know your girlfriend isn't in any trouble tonight, are ya coming back to the apartment?" Ernie asked.

"Why? Do you miss me," I laughed.

"Quite the opposite, actually! I'm trying to decide whether or not to order porn so..." Ernie left the question in the air.

At that moment, Gracie walked out of the bedroom and gave me a tiny smile before heading to the bathroom. She was cute when she first woke up, like a sleepy lioness cub. "No. Ya know what, knock yourself out. Just do me a favor and be clean about your night off."

"Of course," Ernie accepted the terms.

"Anything else?" I asked.

"Oh yeah, your mom says, "Hello" and wants you to call when you can. Until then, she's got us covered in New York," Ernie added.

I nodded, "Perfect!"

"Yeah, I told her what you did. She thinks you're an idiot, too." Ernie informed me before hanging up.

When Gracie came out of the bathroom, I hoped things would be back to normal. She looked me in the eyes and smiled I started the coffee. "I hope you like it strong," I told her.

"Strong is wonderful, thank you," she said as she grabbed a coffee cup.

"Oh, I washed your favorite cup for you," I grabbed it out of the dish strainer.

Gracie cocked her head, "How do you know it's my favorite?" she asked after I handed it to her.

I thought as quickly as I could, "I just assumed. It's a Capricorn cup and I know you like to read your horoscope. Plus, it was the only one in the sink besides mine."

She nodded at me, but I wasn't sure she bought my explanation. "So now you have a cup?" she grinned at me.

"Well, one that I used," I grinned back. It seemed like all the weirdness between us last night was gone and I aimed to keep it that way.

CHAPTER 25

GOOD MORNING GRACIE

I decided that whatever had happened last night, I refused to feel embarrassed around Fall. I had a temporary moment of weakness...cleverly disguised *needing*, that's all, nothing more than that. Given my *lack of* for well over a year and a half, I'd be this attracted to any man I was that close to, I told myself. I tried not to poke holes in this thought as I had never been attracted to anyone I worked on, and they were naked on my table. Okay, dammit, maybe it was him; but I refused to make an uncomfortable situation, more so. I finished my bathroom mirror pep talk and went to face him.

I loved seeing him in my kitchen and it made me smile. Then I reminded myself that he was not a boyfriend, or possible love interest. This was not a relationship.

He offered me coffee. This was how I liked to start my mornings. Not that I didn't enjoy breakfast yesterday, it's just not how I would normally do things.

"I washed your favorite cup," he said.

This was odd to me. How would he know that this cup was my favorite? He gave me an excuse about me reading my daily horoscope. I wasn't sure I bought it. But seeing how my radar was apparently *off* these days, I didn't want to try and read too much into it.

"So I talked to Ernie," he said. "I'm gonna be here till at least tomorrow. I hope that's not too much of an imposition for you?"

"That's fine," I said. "Any more news," I asked.

He gave me the grin and then shook his head. So yes, there was news, just none that he could share with me. Lovely!

"So, aside from coffee, what else do you do in the morning?" Fall asked.

I bit my bottom lip, he saw this and grinned. "No...it's weird," I told him.

"What?" he asked. "What do you do?" he asked again, with a teasing tone.

"I..." it was going to sound stupid that I considered *dancing* exercise. He was staring at me with a half grin. "I exercise," I answered.

"Why is that weird? Do you usually go to the gym?" he wanted to know.

I shook my head, "I don't have a gym membership."

"Oh, you probably use the gym in the rec-room, right?"

I shook my head again, "No I usually do it here."

He looked around the room: no exercise equipment, no weights, not even a yoga ball, "What kind of exercise do you do?"

"You know I really don't have to. I mean a couple of days isn't gonna throw me off. I'll just find something else to do. No big deal."

"No, seriously, I want you to go on about your normal life. I don't want you to feel like you can't do everything you would usually do."

"Except go outside," I threw it out there.

"Yeah, except that," he agreed. "So what do you do? Yoga? Pilates?

I, um, well...I dance," I said.

His grin got wider, "You dance?" he asked folding his arms across his chest. "What kind of dancing?"

"I don't know, I just dance," I answered.

"Like, hip-hop or modern?"

"Uh, no, not exactly."

"Tap?"

"Nooo."

"Polka?" he laughed.

"Yes. I do polka," I said straight faced.

"Really?" he furrowed his brow.

"No," I shook my head.

"Well then what kind?" he flashed his winning smile. "You can tell me."

"Kinda...a cross between... a Salsa..."

His brows lifted.

"...and belly dancing," I took a sip of my coffee and looked away from him.

He rubbed his bottom lip with his thumb, and there it was, one of the sexiest things I've ever seen.

"You Salsa!" it wasn't a question.

"Well, that's the closest thing I can compare it to. It works all your muscle groups," I added as a lame add-on to my visible self-consciousness.

He nodded slowly, still lining his lip with his thumb, "I bet. That sounds, uh..."

"Stupid," I cut him off.

"Yeah, that's not where I was going with that," he shook his head.

We both just stared at each other for a moment.

"I imagine you'll want some privacy to..." he cleared his throat and looked away from me, "dance."

"I'd prefer it," I admitted. "I only need about thirty minutes."

"Well, uh, I can go take a shower, and then you can dance your heart out," he offered.

"I thought you took a shower last night?" I cocked my head at him.

"Yeah, I think I could use another one," his head nodded.

I looked at him sidelong. "Okay. Then I'm going to go change," I said, actually grateful not to be missing too much of my workout while on *vacation*.

I went to my bedroom to change into what I wore to dance in: yoga pants and a tank top. I pulled out the pants Krissy had given me for Christmas last year, and shook my head NO. There was no way I was wearing tight yoga pants that had SEXY spelled out across the ass. I had a hard time wearing them when it was just me in the house. I threw on a pair of plain black yoga pants and a white tank top. I heard the shower go on again and figured I was in the clear to start my workout.

Standing in the living room, I clipped my iPod onto my pants. Putting in my earbuds, I began with some deep stretches. As uncomfortable as I felt doing this with a man in the house (especially a drop-dead-gorgeous one), all of my thoughts and nervousness started to fade as the music carried me away.

The sensual sound of the drum's rhythm, the *ting* of the cymbals ran down my spine. As the speed increased, so did my hip movements. Every muscle was stretching. My breathing was intensifying; sweat was running down my chest and back as my pelvic bone thrust forward and backward. I concentrated on the feeling as my hips moved in a continuous eternity symbol. Up, down, up, down, they shook as I threw my head back and enjoyed how alive my body felt. Bringing my hands over my head in a stretch, and then down to my toes, I pushed my glutes into the air and pumped. As I opened my eyes, there he stood, staring, upside down from my point of view. I jumped up and did a 180 all in one move.

"What the hell?" I said.

He looked just as shocked as he mouthed something at me. Pulling my earbuds out, I asked "What?"

"I'm sorry," Fall said. "Your phone was ringing."

I wondered how much he had seen as I grabbed my hand towel and patted the sweat running down my neck.

"The phone was in the bathroom?" I asked, confused.

"Yeah, I had to make a call and my cell was dead. When I hung up it started ringing. It read "*SIS*" on the readout," his face was red as he rambled on, "I didn't know if it was important and if you needed to call her back right away or if it was nothing..."

I grinned at his reaction, "It's okay. I'll call her back after I get out of the shower," I breezed past him and into the bathroom.

CHAPTER 26

JUST ENOUGH TIME

My first call I asked to see if my background information had been accessed in the last 24 hours. As I waited on hold, I tried to convince myself that my classified information was safe. Most people would only get the basics, where I was born, birth date, marital status and whether I had any felony arrests.

"Yes it looks like it was accessed at 1pm yesterday, but only basic information was released due to a lack of clearance. Is there anything else I can do for you, agent Linn?" the operator asked.

"No. Thank you," I hung up. If she had tried to access my past in any way, it wouldn't be very revealing. But if she had her husband access my information from a department computer, it would come up as classified information and ask for clearance. Then he, and most likely she, would know something was up.

20 minutes left. That gave me enough time hopefully. The phone call I had to make was going to take a little time to explain. I hope I'm doing the right thing, I thought as I dialed the number.

As I hung up, the phone in my hand began to ring. Incoming call from "***SIS"*** showed on the display.

She hadn't spoken much about her sister, but I had listened to a few calls. I knew whatever it was, was probably just her sister venting to her. But what if it wasn't?

I wet my head so it looked like I had been in the shower. Opening the door, I didn't hear any music. Was she done? I called out to her...nothing. There's no way she wouldn't have heard me. Did she leave? Panicked, I hurried to the living room. There she was, her glutes pushed up to the heavens, pumping up and down. Shit...I was going to need another shower, I thought. She was hypnotic to watch as I turned my head right and left then right again, following the movement of her hips. Finally she looked through her legs and saw me. I jumped, it was an immediate response to being caught being *pervy*. She had earbuds in and couldn't hear me as I began to babble. Why did I come out here again? My brain searched for the answer.

Ah, "Your sister called," I said, rambling like an idiot.

She was covered in sweat, her breathing hard. I had seen her this way in dreams. She passed by me and said something that still didn't register until she went to the bathroom and closed the door behind her.

CHAPTER 27

THE MORON COMETH

"What we do with body?" Amsel asked.

"It cannot be found in room I rented!" Knushka found the elevator operator's keys in his pocket. One key had *SERVICE* printed across it.

"But you rent under assumed name?" Amsel tried to reason.

"Yes, but face on security camera...is Knushka," Knushka tried to explain to his brain dead nephew. "You get problem, here?"

"I know this," Amsel said, his face showing clearly that he was not even sure what he was supposed to know.

"You will go to laundry room. Get cart and maid uniform," Knushka explained.

"Right," Amsel nodded, but didn't move.

"You go now!" he added.

"I wasn't sure, I could have done after we eat, or before I shower..." Amsel offered.

Losing it, Knushka hit him with a towel as he yelled, "Now, now, now! I mean now! We handle NOW!"

Amsel returned with the cart and a uniform that wouldn't fit...him. Holding up the uniform, Knushka asked, "Why you bring such small uniform?"

"It fits you," Amsel explained.

"But was supposed to fit you," Knushka said.

"You no said that," Amsel shook his head.

Knushka, wearing the gray maid's uniform dress and his wingtips with black socks, hid his face from the camera as he pushed the cart filled with sheets, pillowcases and the dead body of the elevator operator to the service elevator. He tried the key and the service elevator opened. Down in the hotel's basement, among the heating and plumbing pipes, Knushka found the industrial trash crusher. Wrapping the body in the sheets, he wrestled it into its new hiding place. Wiping the cart clean of all prints and changing into the suit he had hidden under the sheets, he stomped, out of breath, back up the stairs.

"We have breakfast?" Amsel asked.

Knushka, at the end of his rope, the one he wanted to put around Amsel's neck, said through a tightened jaw, "We get the hell out of here, you moron!"

CHAPTER 28

A WOMAN'S INTUITION

Krissy waited for Nate to get off the phone then plated his breakfast.

Nate sat and barely looked at his wife as he put a spoonful of sugar in his coffee.

Krissy's eyes slit as she watched her husband, "What's up?" she asked suspiciously.

"What? Nothing! Why?" Nate panicked.

"You look...strange," Kris eyed him closely.

Nate knew he couldn't lie to his wife. Not well, at least. And anytime he tried to keep anything from her, the guilt of trying would give him away. He had never successfully surprised her with anything, not a gift, a vacation, a surprise party, nothing.

Krissy stared at her husband some more.

"I just need to eat and get to work. It's just gonna be a long day. That's all," Nate shook his head.

"Fine," Krissy said then sat down and watched with the *I know what you've done* look that had worked so many times in the past.

Nate ate as quickly as he could, kissed his wife and all but ran for the door.

After the door closed, Krissy laughed to the heavens, "Oh, I've got him running...just a matter of time, baby!" she smiled.

CHAPTER 29

BIG DEALS AND DUMBASS'S

Knushka's limo drove to the warehouse on the New York Harbor. Amsel sat quietly pouting over being reprimanded. As the limo parked, Knushka explained to his nephew, "You are not to speak."

"Unless spoken to?" Amsel asked.

"I am quite certain that this will not be an issue," Knushka informed him.

Walking into the warehouse Knushka was approached by two armed guards.

Slovak noticed Knushka's arrival and told his guards, "Stand down."

Slovak was a tall, balding man in his sixties, with a muscular build who always wore a turtleneck to hide the large scar on his throat from a botched assignation attempt.

The guards both looked at their boss with questioning eyes.

"This is my oldest friend," Slovak told them. "There is no need to search him."

Knushka smiled as he and Slovak embraced.

"You'll have to forgive my security." Leaning close to Knushka's ear, he said, "My nephews. Dumb as rocks."

Knushka nodded to his old friend and gestured to Amsel, "My nephew," his head shook.

"What have we done to be blessed with such stupidity?" Slovak asked.

Knushka shook his head again, "Is price I pay to keep the family in business."

"You dream of killing him?" Slovak asked, quietly.

"Everyday," Knushka said as he and Slovak tried to figure out which of the three was the dumbest.

"Come, we drink, then do business," Slovak said in the thick Russian accent that never left him.

CHAPTER 30

NO WORDS NEEDED

"Wow, you don't say," this was the first time Gracie had spoken since dialing her sister's number ten minutes ago.

I tried my best not to laugh, as her eyes rounded. Apparently she hadn't exaggerated about their very one sided conversations. Another ten minutes passed and she said, "Right," followed closely by "Okay, I love you, too."

Hanging up the phone she turned and let out a long held breath.

"Everything okay?" I asked.

"Yeah, I guess my nephew colored on the fridge," Grace shook her head.

"That's not good," I said.

"No, what's not good is the fact that her husband was supposed to be watching him. What's even worse is what he drew."

"I can't imagine," I confessed.

"Well, he drew a tall angry woman, and two dwarfed men running away for her."

My eyes rounded as I tried not to laugh at the mental image.

"I guess she asked him who the drawing was of, and he

pointed out mommy as the angry woman. Then, he pointed to the dwarfed men and said, "And that's me and daddy...running away from you."

"Oh, damn!" I said.

"Yeah, then her husband laughed," Gracie lifted her brows and tried not to laugh.

"I'm guessing he's in the doghouse?" I asked.

"Doghouse implies that he will be left in peace to think of what he's done. He's not that lucky," she said. "He's in the *be berated* until *you feel bad for what you've done* house.

I winced, "That sounds like a little slice of hell."

CHAPTER 31

TRY NOT TO LAUGH

I was on the phone with my sister. It seems my three year old nephew was in trouble, again, and it was his father's fault...again. I keep catching Fall stealing glances of me. But doesn't that mean I was doing the same thing? What did all these glances mean? I knew why I looked; he was drop dead gorgeous. But why did he keep staring at me? I wondered. Maybe because there was nothing else to do here, I figured.

I suggested another movie marathon to pass the time.

CHAPTER 32

ONE WAY OR ANOTHER

Krissy's ass swung from side to side as she sashayed into the police department. She knew there was more than one way to skin a cat. Her husband's fellow officers had a hard time keeping their stares to a respectful glance. Dressed in a black pencil skirt, form fitted red top (that left no question as to how great her form was), and pouty red lips, she asked the officer at front desk if her husband was busy.

Nate stepped out of his cubicle, took one look at his wife and mumbled under his breath, "Oh shit."

Krissy grinned at his response. I have him now, she thought. Kris and Nate's marriage was the stuff legends were made of. Everyone who ever knew Nate, knew that Kris had been his drug of choice since grade school.

When she walked into the police department looking like sex-in-spiked-heels, cheeks rose. When she said she needed a moment alone with her husband, no one, including Nate, thought there was any chance they were going to do any talking.

"Um, we can talk in the break room," Nate led her down the hallway to the small occupied room.

Seeing the two of them walk in, the other officers willingly took their leave. Kris stood by the door and told the officers who were exiting the room, “I’ll only be a minute.”

Nate could be heard to say, “She means ten.”

Kris smiled at the new recruits, “Yeah, right,” she said, amused at her husband’s imaginings that it would take her that long.

Shutting the door, she walked to where Nate stood, eyes rounded.

CHAPTER 33

THE GOOD OL' DAYS

Knushka was led into what looked like an old bank vault. Pulling the door closed behind them, Slovak pointed to a leather bound wingback chair.

"Sit my friend. Vodka?" Slovak asked, looking over his shoulder.

"Yes, thank you," Knushka said. "Do you ever worry you will be locked in here by Tweedledumb and Tweedledumber?"

Slovak smiled and handed his old friend a drink, "I have made many moderations to the vault BECAUSE I know who I am working with. The lock has been moved to the inside and several scramblers have been used so that they won't hear my discussions. After all, secret keeping is not exactly a talent of those blessed with stupidity. Is why I never used your name. The less they know...the better," his Russian accent thick.

Knushka made a face, he was sure that Amsel, even though told not to speak, most likely would. "Someday, my nephew will become one of those loose ends that must be tied." Knushka made a throat cutting gesture.

Slovak nodded, "I know what you mean," he held out his glass and toasted to the shared foresight.

"So, you have received documents?" Knushka asked.

"I have, this will make many happy...and the two of us, very rich," Slovak sat back in his chair.

"You have buyers?" Knushka asked.

"Already waiting. Soon they will have new lives. But, my friend, I would be remiss if I didn't inform you that the FBI, several different departments have been sniffing around. Asking questions," Slovak's stare was one of warning.

"This has been brought to my attention as well. I will be unable to bring people across. But, will find another way. There is always another way," Knushka laughed.

"You know they are now talking of fingerprint recognition to fly? It's years off, I believe, but it will complicate our work, no matter when it is enabled."

"Hopefully, that will be a problem for our sons, if not grandsons," Knushka lifted his glass to his friend.

"It is becoming harder and harder to be entrepreneur," Slovak shook his head.

Knushka smiled, "With this last haul, I may let son have business. Maybe use one of my new identities to take up bocce ball in Italy."

"You are warhorse, I doubt you will ever retire," Slovak grinned.

CHAPTER 34

TO LIE...OR NOT TO LIE

My eyes bugged out of my head when I saw '*Mom*' flash across my phone's screen.

"Oh my God, what do I do?" I asked Fall.

He looked at the name, "What's the problem?"

"I can't lie to my mother," my head shook furiously.

"Why would she ask about me?" he tried to reason.

"What if Krissy told her she called me and some guy was here?" I shot back a question.

Fall hadn't thought of that. "What if you just don't answer the call," he winced, knowing how close I was to my mother.

"If there is a man in my home that she has never heard of, and I don't answer, she'll be here in an hour and a half!" I explained.

"So what do we do? You can't tell her!" Fall tried to reason.

"Go outside," I told him as the phone stopped ringing.

"It stopped ringing," his eyes huge.

"She's gonna call right back," I said as the phone in my hand began to ring. "Seriously go outside. That way if I say you aren't here, it's mostly true."

"Damn, you really can't lie to your mom, can you?" he asked slipping out the front door.

"Hi mom," I said as normally as possible when the door closed behind Fall.

"Hi honey, did I catch you indisposed?" she asked.

Why she couldn't just ask me if I was in the bathroom was beyond me, but we all had our own things. "What's up?"

"I got the strangest call from Kris. She said that she called yesterday and there was some man there."

"Ugh, yeah, that's one of my...friends." I stumbled over the word a little, but justified it by thinking that we WERE getting to know each other, and he was here to protect me; what else do friends do, right?

"Oh, I haven't heard of him," mom sounded hurt, like I was purposely keeping her out of the loop.

"I just met him very recently...here at the apartment," I winced. Such a stretch, I thought to myself.

"Oh, so you aren't having a secret life that you're keeping from me? That makes me feel better. So, is this a romantic possibility?" mom searched.

I looked at the closed door and sighed, "I don't think so."

"Well, that sigh makes me question...why not?"

"I don't think he thinks of me that way. I thought he was interested...but then, it seems I was mistaken."

"Well, if there is a man out there that doesn't see how amazing you are, he's not worth your time," she said matter-of-factly.

Oh, the things mothers tell their daughters, I thought. "I know mom, he's just...amazing himself," I said.

"Well, I just wanted to make sure everything is okay. Ya know Kris was talking about having a background check ran on him," she laughed.

My eyes rounded, I knew this was a real possibility. "Everything is fine," I told her. Even though, with this new verification of Kris's intentions I was worried.

"Okay, baby, I love you," she told me.

"I love you, too, mom." I hung up and knocked on the door to let Fall know he could come back in.

"How'd it go?" Fall asked, shutting the door behind him.

"Well, I did have to tell her there was a man here. Turns out that Krissy did call her. I didn't give her a name, though."

"Good," he sighed.

I started shaking my head, "Not really. Krissy is having a background check ran on you," I informed him.

"It's okay," Fall put his hand on my shoulder and looked deep into my eyes. "I already took care of that."

"Is she in danger," I asked, my heart pounding.

"No. As long as she's away from here, she's completely safe," he nodded. "And as long as I'm here, so are you," his eyes burned with intensity.

I nodded. The reality of what was happening, or what could happen, was something I couldn't prepare for. I had no information that would help me understand just where the danger was coming from. The uneasy feeling that had somewhat left me, was back. And, should something happen...my mother would know I kind of lied to her. Suddenly I had this vision of me tied to a spit, roasting over a raging fire...in hell.

CHAPTER 35

FALL FOR GRACE

I knew that Grace's conversation with her mother was being recorded. If anything was alarming, Ernie would notify me immediately. I had to admit, meeting a woman who was afraid of lying to her mother was a breath of fresh air. Fall grinned at how cute Grace was when she said, "I can't lie to my mother."

CHAPTER 36

SLIGHT OF HAND

Slovak hung up the phone, “We have problem,” he said to Knushka.

Knushka lifted one eyebrow, “Explain.”

“There are eyes on your plane. They know you are here. That is going to make harder to get back to Oregon to pick up final package.”

Knushka cussed in Russian. “Why can’t they just let the working man do his job!” his fist slammed down on the table.

“I have plan,” Slovak told him. “Plan will help me as well,” his smile was sinister.

CHAPTER 37

THE WEAPON OF CHOICE

Nate sat in a rolling chair, his pants unbuttoned and thoroughly out of breath. "We need one of these chairs," he told his wife.

Kris grinned as she finished reapplying her lipstick. Walking over to her husband and licking her upper lip, she asked, "Is there anything you need to tell me?" she said in a low seductive manner.

Nate swallowed hard, "Uh...I love you."

"Mmm, I love you too," she leaned in and nuzzled his ear, "Anything else," she whispered.

Nate's eyes had closed with the action his ear was receiving. "I...I...," goose pimples rising on his flesh.

"Yes baby," she said slowly.

"I need new boxers," he blurted out.

Kris leaned back to look into his eyes, her own, slit, "Is that all you have to tell me?"

Nate swallowed hard again, "Yes...and the *I love you*, thing."

Kris stuck her tongue in her cheek and stood, "Okay baby...I'll see you at home."

As she strutted to the door and waved goodbye, Nate was frightened. It was going to be a long night.

CHAPTER 38

IT JUST MIGHT WORK

Knushka stared at Slovak's two nephews. If it weren't winter, this plan would have no chance. Tweedledumb, was tall and thin with shoulder length black hair. He would easily pass for Amsel in a trench coat, hat, dark glasses with a scarf wrapped around his neck. Tweedledummer was shorter, a little heavier but that was all muscle, Knushka told himself. If the scarf was wrapped high enough...dark glasses and a hat...yes, he would pass. He knew he had nothing to fear if officers did stop him. The transaction had been made here. What he didn't want was eyes on him in Oregon, where a package that could put him away forever waited for him.

"Two birds," Slovak said, "They will track your plane back to Russia, and you can go on to Oregon unnoticed. I will have a trusted friend's jet take you to Oregon and bring you back, all under radar. And best part of the plan, my nephews go back to Russia, and I no have to kill them," he grinned.

Knushka nodded, "I am liking this plan. Too bad my nephew can't ride back with them," he laughed.

"We will have your plane leave tonight. They," he pointed to his nephews, "will stay secluded between the plane, limo and warehouse in Russia. Should give you ample time to get in, do what you need, and have safe exit. We make sure eyes have moved back to Russia and send you tomorrow morning. This works for you?"

Knushka smiled and hugged his old friend, "This works for me."

Slovak nodded, "And now…we drink!"

CHAPTER 39

PREOCCUPATION

She seemed really worried now, Fall thought. Gracie's demeanor had changed since talking to her mom. She seemed to be lost in thought. I hated that she was wrapped up in this. I hated that I had...I was the one who put that fear in her eyes.

"So what do you want to watch?" I asked, hoping to take her mind away from her possible reality.

She stared directly ahead at the green tree covered mountain her apartment window faced, "Something by Disney," she said.

CHAPTER 40

THE LONG NIGHT COMETH

Nate was supposed to be home at four. Kris sat at the kitchen table with nothing on but a frilly apron, heels and lipstick. She knew he couldn't avoid her for long. She also knew she couldn't just sit here much longer unless she turned up the heat. Her nipples were at *glass-cutting* attention.

As she heard his car pull up she looked at the clock. 4:55pm and he was about to be given the ride of his life. A smile stretched across her face, "I have something warm for you," said as he came through the door (which of course was a lie by now).

CHAPTER 41

SAY HELLO TO MOTHER RUSSIA

Slovak received the call from one of his many informants in New York; the plane had lifted off and the agents had followed.

"You will wait few more hours to make sure ALL eyes have turned to Russia," Slovak said.

"Thank you, old friend," Knushka said. Putting his feet up on the ottoman and relaxing, he said, "We have done this for so many years, you would think they would think us ghosts by now."

Slovak smiled, "Remember the bikers?"

Knushka almost spit out his Vodka, "I had all but forgotten of this! What good times we have had. And you remember hobbling that one with the scary face...you made him cry like baby."

"Remember his pleading...'*Please, I have wife and children*', even though moments before he was to say, "*I will kill you...wife...children*!" It still makes me happy to think of tables turning," Slovak shook his head at the memory.

Knushka's smile faded a little, "But Demeter...ah."

Slovak nodded slowly, "You had no choice, dear friend. Some offenses...demand punishment."

Knushka nodded as well.

"Here," Slovak raised his glass, "we will toast him...it will do your soul well," he told his friend. "To Demeter!"

"To Demeter," Knushka said and they took their shots down.

CHAPTER 42

A LITTLE MORE INFORMATION, A LITTLE LESS ACTION?

"I have to take this," I told Grace.

Stepping into the bedroom, I answered the phone, "What's up, Ernie?"

"I just received a call from your mother," Ernie said.

"What's going on?"

"It seems that Knushka is headed back to Russia. His plane just took off."

I rolled this around in my head, "Are they sure it was Knushka's plane?" I asked.

"They're positive, buddy," Ernie sounded as confused as I felt.

"Are they positive that Knushka's on the plane?"

"They have pictures of him and his nitwit nephew boarding the plane. It looks legit according to our sources," Ernie added.

"You think maybe he caught wind of the ***eyes*** on him here, and aborted?" I asked.

"It's possible. He hasn't evaded paying for his crimes all these years by taking unnecessary risks."

"And you're sure that guy that was at Grace's, the handyman, didn't retrieve the package...and isn't on Knushka's payroll?" I asked again for confirmation.

"We checked the guy, his car, his background...not to mention we've had *eyes* on him since he left the parking lot. The guy's a dead end," Ernie confirmed. "You're sure it's not in the apartment?"

"I've looked. I can't even imagine where it would be. But...I'll keep looking, as long as I don't raise Grace's suspicions. She's nervous enough. I can't go tearing her house apart without making things worse for her."

"So, does that mean you're not coming back tonight either?" Ernie questioned.

"Well, until we're one-hundred-percent..." I reasoned.

"RRRIIIGGGHHHT," Ernie said.

"...And we're about to order Chinese food...it would be rude to leave now."

"So...I can order pay-per-view, then?" Ernie asked.

"Why don't you go home and sleep with your wife?" I laughed.

"Nah, she doesn't really like me that way."

I shook my head and laughed, "Okay. Well then, I'll leave you to it," I let him know.

"Oh, one more thing before you hang up," Ernie called into the receiver.

"Yeah?"

"Your little girlfriend...wants you."

My heart pounded harder, "What do you mean?"

"I recorded that conversation...the one she had with her mother..."

"Yeah?" All I could think of was, he better not be fucking with me.

"Yeah, she said something about you not liking her, her thinking you did, then not thinking you did...and how she hoped you did...something like that," Ernie babbled.

"Why the hell didn't you tell me that?" I blurted out.

"Well, gee...I was a little busy with the FBI, CIA, NYPD. and the OCI, to send you a text with your names written in a big red heart. Forgive me," Ernie let his sarcasm fly.

"You're right," I shook my head, "I'm sorry. You've actually more than held up my end of the investigation. I owe you."

"Don't bother me while I watch just who Debbie does in Dallas, and we're even," Ernie hung up.

It was almost hard to breath...she likes me? And Ernie watches really old porn.

CHAPTER 43

FEAR BEGETS FEAR, BEGETS FEAR, BEGETS FEAR

Fall had been on the phone for a long time. Or at least the longest he had been. I was more than nervous, picking at my cuticles. What kind of danger was I in? From who...the question still boggled my brain. I knew no one in this town, at least, not anyone who was...a *bad seed.* Is that what they call it? Why do they call it that? My mind had derailed. I think it was its defense mechanism. My mind during times of great stress...just shuts down.

Fall walked back into the living room where I had half-heartedly been watching *Shrek.* He was smiling. Smiling was a good thing, right?

"Good news," Fall said, "Looks like the danger has moved far, far away from you."

"Seriously?" I asked, letting out a deep breath then jumping into his arms. "Thank you for being here," I kissed his cheek.

"Yep," he smiled at my reaction. "So...um...I can leave now."

"Oh, right," I let go of him and took a couple of steps back. I hadn't thought of that. Once the danger was gone...he would be, too.

"Or..." Fall started.

My eyebrows arched, "Or?"

"Even though I have it on good authority that all is well…I would like to stay for awhile. Just to make sure, ya know? Just seems like the right thing to do."

I smiled.

"One more night…if you don't mind," he added, "…would just make me feel better," he shrugged.

I nodded, "Chinese food?"

CHAPTER 44

TOO MUCH OF A GREAT THING

Rolling off of Nate for the second time, Kris and her husband panted in unison. Determined to get the information she needed, she had been willing to go all night. Sex had always been her weapon of choice and he had always been her favorite form of torture.

Grabbing her by the hand, Nate brought it to his lips for a kiss. "You," he breathed, "you are incredible."

Grinning, Kris told him, "So are you, my love." The smile on her face was marked by the clear exhaustion that physical satisfaction brings.

Nate curled up into his normal sleep position; on his side facing her, with one hand on her boob.

"What are you doing?" Kris asked.

"I need to sleep, baby. I'm beyond worn," he smiled at his bride.

"Baby, do you have anything you want to tell me?" Kris looked him in the eyes.

She noticed that Nate became flustered and was having trouble meeting his wife's stare. She knew it wasn't another woman. Of all the things she was certain about in this lifetime, she was most certain of this. So what was he hiding? It wasn't her birthday. They didn't have money for a trip, but their bank account wasn't in trouble, either. He had just passed his physical, so he wasn't sick.

"I love you," he said with heartfelt devotion.

"And I, you. Anything else?" her voice hinting suspicion.

"It's nothing honey, I'm just tired," he leaned in and kissed her cheek.

Kris's eyes slit, wrong answer, she thought. Mounting him, she told him, "We'll see if the *third time* IS *a charm*."

Nate whimpered, "Oh God..."

CHAPTER 45

GOOD FORTUNE, WILL BE YOURS

As we waited for the Chinese food to be delivered, we finished watching Shrek. I know that it was weird that I had a pang of...I-don't-even-know-what when I thought about Fall leaving. I wasn't scared. Well, not really...anymore. I had enjoyed him being here. And even though I never thought of myself as some damsel-in-distress (far from it), I knew that he was here to protect me and something about his desire to do so, the selflessness, was sexy. I knew it had to be part of the job, but was it always like this for him? Did he always connect to the ones he was protecting? Some part of me didn't think this was true. Or, maybe that's just what I wanted to think.

"So I say we watch *Shrek 2* when the food gets here?" he said.

"Sounds good," I smiled.

I did wonder if I could now ask what had been going on, that put me in danger. I mean, if I was no longer in danger, wouldn't he be able to tell me?

"Fall?" I started.

He smiled when I said his name, "Yes Grace."

"Now that the danger is gone, can you tell me what was happening?" I asked him.

"Ya know, I think I can. I can't give you all the specifics, but I can give you the gist," his brown eyes sparkled. He turned toward me, "You know your neighbor...your downstairs neighbor?"

I thought for a moment, "The Russian gentleman?" I cocked my head.

"Right," Fall licked his lips, "he's been receiving packages...from all over the world."

I nodded. I had had some of them in my possession from time to time. "Right!"

"Those packages are the link to his Russian Crime affiliation," Fall said seriously.

"He's part of a Russian Crime syndicate?" I said more to myself than him. "And I was in danger..."

"Because you received and held the packages for him, when he was out of the country," Fall informed me. "It's also why you've been on our radar...and why we knew you needed protecting."

"You really think he would have...hurt me?" I didn't have the heart to say the 'K' word.

"Knushka is well known...for never leaving a loose end," Fall watched to see how I would respond to this knowledge.

"Oh my God," I stood and began to pace. "That nice old man?"

"Grace, you're safe. He's gone." Fall stood and put his arms around me, "And even if he wasn't, I wouldn't let anything happen to you."

I nodded with my head against his chest. I still couldn't picture it...that sweet old man...was Russian Mafia...and a killer.

"The package," I blurted out.

"That's what I was doing in here when you surprised me," Fall explained.

"I surprised you?" I shook my head. "But the package, I still have it!"

"You do?" Fall's eyes bugged out. "Where?"

"Well, I had it under the couch..."

"I checked under the couch," he gave me a palms-up, then got down on his knees to inspect under my slip cover.

"No, I moved it!" I told him.

"Where? Where did you move it to?" he showed me his palms again.

"It's in my washing nook," I pointed to where my washer/dryer combo lived.

"I already looked there," his brow furrowed.

"I moved it when you spilled the coffee...when you were getting the paper towels. No offense, but just in case you were even clumsier than me..." I cocked my head and let my thought trail off.

Fall grabbed me by the face and kissed my lips hard and quick, "Thank God you didn't trust me," he said and headed for my washer nook.

I gave him a shocked smile and let out a laugh. So now, was it really done? Now that they had the evidence they needed, was I really safe from my Russian neighbor...the Mafia killer?

Pulling out the package he let out a deep sigh of relief and turned a grin to the heavens. "I have to call Ernie," he ran down the hallway like a happy overgrown child as I laughed behind him.

CHAPTER 46

PORNUS INTERRUPTUS

"Seriously, Fall? You could kill a wet dream. If you want pointers...I'm a little old-school. Just so you know."

"Yeah, I could tell by your choice of porn. Look, Grace had the package the whole time," I laughed.

"And you couldn't find it in her tiny apartment?" Ernie was trying to find the logic. "Is she a hoarder? What is she a complete slob, or something?"

"No, she moved it from one place I didn't look, to someplace I already had," Fall laughed.

"You mean you never just came out and asked her about the package?"

"Of course not, that could have put her in more danger if she knew anything about Knushka."

"Okay," Ernie said, making it clear he would have handled it differently. "So, I take it she knows about him now?"

"Sure, well somewhat," I admitted. "I let her know who the danger was from and that he didn't leave loose ends. I didn't tell her what's in the package."

"Good, I guess. The plane should be landing in Russia in a few hours. We'll have more *eyes* to make a 100% verification that it IS Knushka. I'll call as soon as I know."

"Think I should take the package in right now?" Fall wondered out loud.

"Don't bother. Carter isn't back from San Francisco until tomorrow. It's better off in your care than in an evidence room at the P.D. You don't know who's on Knushka's payroll."

"You're right," Fall nodded. "The Russian crime syndicate had eyes everywhere due to very deep pockets and favors owed from favors needed."

"So now, may I go back to my porn?" Ernie asked.

"Knock yourself out," Fall shook his head.

"Hey there's an Irish joke about that," Ernie started.

"Goodnight Ernie," Fall hung up.

CHAPTER 47

NEVER SAY FRICTION BURN

Crawling off of her husband for the third time, both of them looked like they had been ridden hard and put away wet.

"Do you have anything you'd like to tell me now," Kris panted.

"Please God, no more, I'm raw!" Nate begged her.

Kris, for the first time, was willing to admit defeat...and go to the freezer for an icepack. Whatever he didn't want her to know, had to be big if he could keep his lips tight after all of this. What could it be she wondered, worry starting to creep in.

CHAPTER 48

MOTHER RUSSIA

As the plane touched down in Russia, *eyes* were everywhere. Pictures were taken from a safe distance using zoom lenses. Those pictures were sent back to an agent in New York, Miss Anya Linn.

Many times she had pushed back her retirement when her white whale, Dmitri Knushka, slipped away, again. For the last ten years she had seen the wreckage he had made of her city and the carnage he had left behind. Dead bodies littered the New York streets. Gang wars had become more common with the influx of crime families. And how they killed, told you who they were. Each had their own brand of retribution. Gangs flooded in under the guise of false identification. Dmitri Knushka was helping this reality along by offering these *new identities* to those who would normally stand trial for their sins in their own country. Laying low, staying with their own, they could disappear forever into the crowded U.S. streets. Anya Linn had no problem with immigration being an immigrant herself, from Scotland. But these weren't good people looking to make a new life in a new country. These were some of the greatest dregs of society. And now, they were her problem.

“The plane just touched down,” a bright eyed young agent told her.

Taking the pictures, Anya frowned, “They’re not very good, are they?” she asked.

“They had heavy coats on. They even kept their glasses on although it was dark when they arrived,” the young man looked over her shoulder.

“What does that tell you, agent Davis, is it?” she looked at his name tag.

“Yes ma’am, I believe it means that we need to get better pictures before we can actually *sign off* on the identity of who exactly these men are.”

“Very good,” Agent Linn told the young man. “Please request a *stand-bye*, and let all the other agents know that we need absolute confirmation before we will sign off on Knushka’s location.”

The young agent nodded and went to follow agent Linn’s orders to a tee.

As she sat staring at the pictures, she became more and more convinced that the man in the photo wasn’t Knushka. Even though the photos were blurry from the distance, movement and a heavy snow falling, she couldn’t see the watch he always wore. The watch he had killed a man over, when he tried to mug him. The watch that had been a wedding gift from Knushka’s now deceased wife. Always worn on his left wrist she noticed that even though there was a gap between his glove and the cuff of his trench coat, the watch appeared to be missing. Looking at pictures taken last week in Portland, the watch was clearly visible. Also, she noted, the cuff of the sleeve on the trench coat seemed shorter in the pictures taken today. Almost like the perfectly tailored clothing he always wore, didn’t quite fit.

CHAPTER 49

OLD FRIENDS

Knushka and Slovak laughed as Knushka told him of his nephew's epic fuck-up in the hotel.

"So you dispose of body, of course," Slovack gave Knushka a palms-up, like this was protocol for them; clean-up after all the mistakes their useless hitters made.

"You know, when younger, I had little patience for stupidity. I knew this. Many died because I had no patience to train and fix screw-ups. Now I know, I have still no patience...I'm just too tired to kill all the stupid people, move body, get rid of body," Knushka pushed his hands out like it was all too much to even think about.

"I know," Slovak poured them two more vodkas. "It almost seems now, that asking for someone be competent and thorough is unheard of. But in our day...you did right, first time, or got knock in the head."

Knushka pointed to the scar at his hairline, and laughed.

"What is that from?" Slovak asked.

"Father had to tell me twice," Knushka and his friend laughed.

"Ah, but your boy, Dmitri Jr. he is knock off of block. He would make any father proud," Slovak raised his glass.

"That he is...and does," Knushka confirmed. "And his mother...would have made great killer...if she could keep legs closed," Knushka laughed again.

"Ironic isn't it?" Slovak nodded. "Open legs, is what kills her."

Knushka nodded, "Maybe we toast her, too."

CHAPTER 50

NOT A CREEPER

When the food had been plated from the little white cartons and the movie had been started, Grace found herself thinking over what Fall had said to her; "You've been on our radar." How long, I wondered, had I been on his radar? And who is *our*? Is this how he knew about the jam? Suddenly and without warning she knew where she knew Fall from.

Almost three months before, the electricity had gone out in the apartment. Since I couldn't even make a cup of coffee, I went down the road to the coffee shop. Sitting there for an hour and feeling guilty for occupying a table during their breakfast rush, I broke down and ordered; two eggs, over medium, bacon crisp, hash browns crisp, sourdough toast and raspberry jam.

The waitress had said, "We may not have any raspberry, but I'll check for you." I thanked her and said, "It's my favorite."

I hadn't seen him, but that was the only way, the only time, this could have happened in the past few months.

I stared at my plate, lost in thought.

"Grace, you okay," Fall asked. "Don't you like the food?"

Of course I liked the food, I thought. It's from the Chinese restaurant I always order from and it's my usual order.

"Uh, yeah," I said. Setting my fork down I turned to look at him. "How long have you been watching me?" I asked.

Fall stopped the fork halfway to his mouth. The look on his face was hard for me to read.

"How do you know so much about me? Did you dig through my trash?" I questioned. "Could you see into my apartment?"

His breathing changed, "No, it's not like that," he put one hand up submissively.

"Then how? How do you know about my favorite coffee cup...where I order my pizza from...what kind of pizza I order?" my eyes rounded. "How did you know I was on vacation this week?"

Fall looked like he was going to be sick. Setting his fork down, he said, "I...had your phone tapped."

My eyes bugged out, "Why? How? I mean, don't you need a reason to tap someone's phone?" I looked at the ground for a stable focus point, while my head spun.

"Well," Fall shifted uneasily. "I got the judge to sign off on the tap by saying...you may be involved."

"Involved? In what?" my heart skipped.

"In the illegal activity that Knushka is involved in," his eyes closed.

Covering my mouth with my hand, I tried to comprehend why he would do this. "Did you...do you...think I was involved?"

Fall's head started to shake, "No, no. It's not like that at all. I was just...I was just worried about the way things could play out. I knew that if I said this to a judge...he wouldn't grant the tap."

"So you had my phone tapped...and listened to my personal conversations," my mind was still spinning.

There was a moment of silence, where I went over some of my most private conversations from the last few months; conversations with Kris and my mother...about my broken heart, about being lonely, but too scared to get back out there...about feeling *broken* to my soul. Suddenly, my cheeks began to burn. The embarrassment showed on my face.

"Oh my God," I whispered. "If you knew I wasn't involved...why did you have my phone tapped? You had to know, Knushka never called me...so why? What did you learn about Knushka from listening to my private conversations?"

Fall's head dropped, "I watched you...every day. I tailed you...from home...to work, the store and home, again. You were a job," he nodded. "I had to find out what role, if any, you played in the packages."

I nodded, this part made sense to me. "But I was under the impression that you and I...it was a chance encounter. That I was just caught up in all of this. But now I know you tapped my phone under the pretense that I was conspiring with him? Now I've been put on radar for possible involvement with this man...because...you...?" I left the question hanging.

"Because he doesn't leave loose ends," Fall's eyes turned to mine.

I rolled this around in my head. I was a job, not a happy accident. Furthermore, he had listened to conversations he knew had nothing to do with his job or the case. He had spied on me. Was he making fun of me when I cried to Kris? Did he laugh when I told her I felt unwanted and invisible?

"Please say something Grace," Fall searched for my eyes, but I couldn't look at him.

"Now that your job is done...I think I'd like you to go," I said, really not sure how I felt.

Fall let out a deep sigh and nodded his head, "Of course." As he stood, he said, "I am glad I finally got to meet you. You're an amazing person."

I stared up at him, trying to fight back the liquid beginning to pool in my eyes, "Don't forget the package."

As the door closed behind him, my tears fell. I felt humiliated, embarrassed and little more concerned that I may now be on a *watch list.* My life had gone from boring to surreal in the matter of a couple of days. The saddest part of all of this was that Fall being here, was the happiest I had been since before I walked in and saw my ex-husband taking his mistress's temperature with his beef thermometer.

Putting the Chinese food in my fridge, I spied another bottle wine that Fall had brought to him by the invisible Ernie. It, of course, was my favorite Cabernet Sauvignon. I had to admit, staring at the bottle, made me wonder; why had he gone through so much trouble to know all of my favorite things? Why had he brought all my favorite things to me? The more I thought about the breakfast with raspberry jam, the pizza (the only one I ever ordered, from the only place I would ever order from), the Chinese food, and my favorite wine; was he trying to make me comfortable? Or was there more to all of this? Was I missing something? Or was I reading too much into this...trying to save face?

I couldn't help but sit down and go over all the conversations I remembered having. After a while, I felt every bit as pathetic as I had assumed I was. Only now, Kris and I weren't the only ones who knew.

Opening my third story balcony door, I noticed that snow had begun to fall. I wanted nothing more than to crack a beer, sit in my patio chair and just watch the flurries dance on the wind. But I remembered, I could be being watched by God only knows who and it made me sick to think about.

CHAPTER 51

SWEET DREAMS, ERNIE

I had no idea what I could be walking in on. Considering how Ernie planned on spending his night off, it could be something that would haunt me forever. I chose to knock instead of just walking in. No answer. I knocked again...again no answer. Worried and unarmed, I opened the door cautiously.

Ernie lay on his cot; a bottle of Scotch, lotion and an empty tissue box lay on the bedside table. I shook my head. At least his boxers were on. It looked like he had partaken in a celebration for one as our stakeout was on hold, if not over.

The agency had rented us a studio apartment, one with our window being aimed at Knushka's living room and balcony. I stared at his darkened apartment. Had he really just given up on a multi-million dollar deal, to escape the possibility of being caught? My update told me ***yes***. My gut told me ***NO***. Knushka had never been caught, but he had also never abandoned a job. He found ways around the obstacles and the eyes that may be watching. He was a master of manipulation.

Watching, my eyes were drawn up to Grace's apartment. Her patio door had opened; I could see her staring off into the falling snow. Normally, she would crack a beer and sit in the cold, just enjoying the blanket the snow made over the rooftops and parked cars. Normally, she would be smiling. I took that from her, I thought. Why hadn't I just told her that I watched her, listened to her, because I had fallen for her? I had fallen in love with Grace Fully. I chuckled to myself, knowing that I didn't tell her because it would have made it sound like I had been stalking her. Which in all truthfulness and according to all of my training, I had been. It's not like I had ever done this before, had ever gotten involved with anyone attached to a case. There was just something about...*her.*

Ernie grunted in his sleep, drawing my attention. When I looked back to Grace's patio, she was gone. And I felt the loss her absence brought in my heart.

CHAPTER 52

A MOTHER'S INTUITION

"I can't keep an investigation going, because you have a hunch, Agent Linn," said her superior.

Anya was more than aware of protocol, but she had real concerns that the men in the photos weren't their suspects.

"I understand what you're saying," Agent Linn said, steadying her nerves, "but if you'll look at the photos one more time, I'm sure you will see..."

Cutting her off, Senior Special Agent Barnes, said, "I've looked at the photos, and all I can say is, a watch? We're supposed to continue an investigation, in Russia, because of a watch?" he threw the photos to his desk and shook his head. "Anya, you're a great agent, but we are only worried about what Knushka does stateside."

"That's my point, I believe he IS stateside," Anya said as calmly as her frustration would allow.

"The photos say otherwise," Special Agent Barnes stared at her with the look that told her no further argument would be considered, much less heard.

"I understand," she gave a curt nod to her superior. "Now that the case is closed, I'd like to take my week vacation as we discussed previously."

The two agents stared at each other. Finally, Agent Barnes sighed, "Fine."

Anya grinned at him then walked around his desk to where he stood.

Agent Barnes took her in an embrace and stared deep into her eyes, "You truly are the most stubborn woman I have ever known."

"Just the way you like me," they kissed long and passionately.

"Tell Fall that I hope to see him soon," Agent Barnes let go of Anya reluctantly. "Anything you'd like me to know before you go?" he asked her.

"I'd mourn you if you died," she winked.

"I love you, too," he said.

CHAPTER 53

FOR LOVE…I HAVE BROKEN MYSELF

Kris watched as Nate slept. She didn't know if sleep was the proper term for what he had fallen into; exhausted, worn and completely drained, summed him up more correctly. She debated waking him, the pain of one more round. But as she stared down at her melted icepack, she knew she couldn't rally. For hours and hours again, she had brought him to the brink, only to stop and then start again. Some called this form of making love *Tantric*. After six hours, Nate referred to it as torture, and she was glad he understood that this WAS the purpose behind the act.

"In the morning," she said to her sleeping husband.

CHAPTER 54

ADVICE

At 3am, Ernie woke and tried to swallow past his alcohol induced cotton-mouth. Looking over at me, he tried to steady his focus.

"What the hell are you doing here," Ernie asked.

Standing, I got Ernie a water bottle from our tiny fridge, "She asked me to leave," I said.

"What happened? I thought you two were on your way to making a porno of your own," Ernie unscrewed the cap on the water bottle and took half of it down in one drink.

I explained the whole incident as Ernie listened as intently as a drunk man can.

"So...you never told her how you feel about her?" Ernie asked.

"I couldn't...I'd sound like a stalker!"

"Well, yeah," Ernie said, like this was a given. "But if you never tell her, you take away even the possibility, no matter how slight, that something may come from this," he shook his drunken head. "Look, let me give you some friendly advice," he hiccupped. "If you really love her...and I know you do...you're better off laying your cards on the table than waiting for a perfect hand to be dealt to you."

Fall stared at his best friend and partner of the last ten years. "You're drunk, Ernie."

"Yeah, I am. I'm also married to the woman of my dreams."

I couldn't help but grin. I knew the only reason he didn't go home, was because Mable was at her mother's for the next few days. Truth be told, Ernie loved his wife more than anything. He joked about her, because it was more acceptable than mooning over how much he missed her. But when Ernie drank, he'd tell anyone and everyone that Mable was his only reason for living. If he was really drunk, he'd tell you the story about how she was engaged to someone else and how he did all kinds of crazy things to win her heart.

Ernie's eyes rolled around and his head fell back. Out cold, he began to snore.

CHAPTER 55

NEW YORK TO PORTLAND

"Okay my friend, is time," Slovak said. "All *eyes* have been removed. I have on good authority that U.S. intelligence thinks you are home in Russia. Surveillance here has been halted."

"Ah," Knushka stretched, "thank you, old friend. On return, I will bring you the last of the documents."

Knushka and Slovak hugged and kissed cheeks.

"Come Amsel," Knushka kicked the side of the cot Amsel had been sleeping on. "We go now!"

Amsel opened one eye and said, "Ten more minutes," then rolled away from Knushka's stare.

Knushka looked like he was about to lose his temper. He called to two of Slovak's men, "You please turn cot over."

The two men raced over and flipped the cot, slamming Amsel to the concrete floor.

"Ouch," Amsel yelled, "was not nice," he rubbed where his scull had bounced off the ground.

"You get up now, or I put bullet in your head," Knushka gave him a choice.

Amsel stood, looking like a kicked puppy and grabbed their luggage.

A full length trench coat, scarf, dark glasses and a fedora, Knushka was ready to finish his journey and take care of whatever ends needed to be snipped.

CHAPTER 56

THE CALL

At 3am, my cell rang, not that I was sleeping really anyway. I smiled as I saw the name illuminated in the dark room; *MOM*.

"Hi Ma," I said.

"Listen to me sweetheart, I'm on my way. I'll be on the 7am flight."

"To Portland?" I asked. "What's up Ma?"

"I don't believe that the person on Knushka's plane...that we followed to Russia is him at all.

My heart started to pound, "Why do you think this, Mom?"

"I have some photos that cause me to question. Then there's always women's intuition."

Fall could almost see his mother's face. He knew her intuition had rolled over tenfold since she was a young bride. "Can't Agent Barnes help?"

"You know he can't. By the way, he sends well wishes," Anya told her son.

"Send them back to him for me." There was a moment of silence between them before Fall asked, "Do you think Grace is in danger?"

"Ah, Grace Fully," Anya began, "I heard about your epic fuck-up."

Mom never minced words, Fall thought.

"You care for this woman?" she asked.

"I do...very much." Hearing myself say it out loud...and to my mother, confirmed to my brain what my heart already knew.

"Then you keep her safe, regardless of protocol," Anya told her son.

"Yes ma'am," I told her. "Do you need me to pick you up from the airport?" I asked.

"Silly boy, you know as well as I, that Barnes has already changed my flight to first class and that there will be a car waiting when I arrive," she said. "You may need to pick me up from somewhere nearby. I can't see being under-the-radar in a vehicle with blackened windows and government plates."

Fall smiled, "I figured."

"Tell me you love me?" mom asked.

"I would mourn you if you died," Fall told her and hung up the phone.

I wanted to believe my mother was wrong, for Grace's sake alone. Before Grace, I wanted nothing more that to take Knushka down. But now I knew that desire was secondary to protecting her. I knew I'd let him walk to save her.

Walking back over to the window I looked up to her balcony. I wondered...how would I keep an eye on her without her knowing I was there? It wasn't like I could tell her that the threat had returned. It sounded like I was making it up, just to invade her life. I had already done enough of that. I had to laugh. I had seriously fucked-up. Not just by being in her home and then holding her there, but by doing all the things she liked. It wasn't a rookie mistake. I wasn't a rookie and knew better, even when I did all those things. By wanting to see her happy, give her her favorite things, I had divulged having too much personal knowledge of her. I was supposed to protect her from afar in the first place, I reminded myself. It just made me uncomfortable to do so now.

CHAPTER 57

WHAT HAVE I DONE?

"Too many questions," I said to no one as I sat on my claw-footed couch with my second beer. First, that nice older gentleman living one story below, was not only involved in criminal activity...he was a murderer. I assume that's what Fall meant when he told me that Knuska didn't *leave loose ends*. How many packages had I held for him in the last ten months? Seven, eight, I guesstimated. Could I be considered an accomplice? I mean, if you commit a crime, unknowingly, are you still considered guilty? And Fall, he had been watching me, tailing me and listening to my conversations...for three months? I rubbed my temple and tried to think of *why*? He couldn't have thought I was involved! A quick background check would have shown where I came from, who I was. No money was ever deposited into my account to show that I was being compensated for my very small part in all of this...what was *THIS*, anyway? I still had no idea what Knushka had done. I knew it was illegal (and frightening to think of how he handled the *leftovers*, which is how I would refer to accomplices), but what? Was he a drug dealer? Where those packages filled with heroin? Did he pirate videos and just severely overreact to being caught? No matter how hard I tried, I couldn't see him as a drug dealer. And, no matter how much I tried to keep my mind on Knushka, my thoughts keep going back to Fall.

Yes, he had invaded my privacy. Not to mention my home and life. But why had he ordered my favorite pizza? Why had he gotten the raspberry jam? I would think his training...as whatever he was...would tell him that doing these things, would alert me. At his age, doing this job, this level of surveillance, no matter what department, you'd think he'd know this much. So why had he gone out of his way to do things my way? Without wanting to, I thought of our pizza night together, learning about each other, sharing. Was any of it real? Was he just getting information he hadn't already been able to get from the wiretap and surveillance? Much without my permission, my mind floated back to our dance. I let out a whimper, "He played Otis," I told my beer. "I love Otis," I took a drink. I thought about the grin he gave when he asked me to dance, the intoxicating scent of him. My eyes fell closed as I remembered how enticing his body felt pressed against mine. I heard myself let out a little moan, and suddenly realized that I almost wished he had been a rapist. No! That was wrong, I reprimanded myself. I did not wish that! I just couldn't help but wish that we had taken that moment a few steps further...like you know, to where your eyes roll back in your head, I thought. I looked at my beer, "You're not making it any easier," I told it. Walking over to my stereo, I pushed *PLAY* and let Otis sing to me for another two beers.

CHAPTER 58

TUPITSA

Amsel asked, "Why we not take our plane?"

Knushka's brow furrowed and he shook his head. Could someone that came from his bloodline, even someone who was half someone else, could he really be this stupid?

"Because, plane was used to throw off FBI, stupid. FBI followed plane to Russia," Knushka made hand gestures like a plane in flight for his stupid nephew, "so they would not be following us!"

Amsel's eyes slit, "But how they know to follow plane?"

Knushka stood there just shaking his head, "We no talk anymore."

As they boarded the plane that would take them secretly to Portland, Oregon, Amsel hit his head on the LOW PASSAGE sign. Knushka had to put a hand against Amsel's back to keep him from falling backward and crushing him. Knushka smiled as he thought about how nice it would have been to watch Amsel fall again.

Taking their seats, Amsel started again with his video game, *dong-ding-dong, dong-ding-dong.*

"What is it with you and that racket? Why you play stupid games?" Knushka asked.

Amsel leaned over and showed Knushka what he was playing; a hit man in an Italian suit and fedora was taking out street informants, cops and agents. He showed Knushka how the game was played. Watching, Knushka laughed as the street informants were killed in various ways when you chose their action of demise. Knushka laughed and laughed, pointing to ones he had done. Soon Knushka took Amsel's phone away from him and spent the next two hours laughing and cussing as he hit or missed his targets.

Amsel sat back, sullen and bored, having lost his game to his uncle, the mob boss.

CHAPTER 59

WAKEY WAKEY

Kris woke and rolled over to look at her sleeping husband. He was curled into the fetal position, protecting his junk from another round of raw lovin'.

Smiling she said, "You're going down."

She decided on coffee first and made her way into the kitchen. Walking reminded her that she was also reeling from her chosen form of interrogation. As she sat waiting for her coffee to brew, she wondered if she should put her icepack back in the freezer. Deciding this would be a good idea she filled her coffee cup then headed back to her bedroom.

Walking into their bedroom, she noticed something was missing; Nate. Just then, she heard the car pull out of the driveway. Running to the living room window, she saw his bronco roll down the street.

Kris's eyes slit and her jaw tightened, "It's on!" she yelled.

CHAPTER 60

MAYBE, BUT PROBABLY NOT

I rolled over and almost fell off the couch. I had fallen asleep listening to Otis on replay. "Coffee," I said to no one, being hit by the fact that no one else was there to make it. Oh, come on, she told herself. It's not like the two days he made me coffee had spoiled me to the point of missing him. Even though, she thought, it was nice to have someone else do something for me.

Married all of those years, I couldn't even count on my husband to take out the trash when it was full. Instead, he would keep shoving it down in the bin until the bag had no choice but to tear. Even then, I was always the one who tried to remove the overfilled bag, just to have its contents litter my clean floor. Turning off Otis, I looked out my window at the blanket of white the snow had left behind. Beautiful, I thought. I couldn't stop myself from wondering if Fall liked the snow. I knew he had been raised here. Or at least, that's what he had said. I can't imagine he would stay if he didn't love Oregon and all of her seasons. Hell, he had been named after one of them.

When I went to open my front door and retrieve my morning paper, I stopped. Should I be wary? Looking out the peephole, I spied no one. No sound or movement. Even though, I only opened my door a crack and shoved my hand out grabbing my rolled news and retreating quickly. Shutting the door, I chastised myself, there was nothing to fear.

Sitting at my island/kitchen table, I read the front page, nothing...nothing about Knushka, nothing about the closing of an investigation. Just more about these falsified documents that were enabling gang members, Mafia and other dregs of society to enter and disappear in the U.S.

Annoyed by politics and bad, even horrifying news, I turned to my horoscope.

CAPRICORN:

Nothing is as it seems; for a Cap, this is torture. You prefer to be kept in the loop and have others deal straight-up with you. You pride yourself on living this way and respect other's who play by the same rules. Sometimes though, being out of the loop is for your own good.

Truthfully, I could apply this to anything, I thought. Now I couldn't help but apply it to the last few days and unwanted information. I told myself I wouldn't read Fall's horoscope. I put the paper down and purposely walked away. Refilling my coffee cup, I sat down and stared at the paper. Frustrated by desire to read Scorpio, I flipped the paper over so I couldn't see the horoscope section.

Diverting my eyes, I looked at everything else in the room. Soon it felt like the paper was calling me, I took sidelong glances at it. Letting out a deep breath, I flipped the paper back over.

SCORPIO:

Someone you care for may have been given the wrong impression of your intentions. Instead of staying silent and

> hoping things work out in your favor, you may have to find a better way to express yourself and your feelings.

I rolled this over in my head, too. It also could apply to anything...so why did it make me wonder if I had missed something important...something he didn't say. "Oh, you're reaching!" I told myself. "Do you really think HIS horoscope is about YOU?" I asked.

I took myself to the bathroom. A nice, long hot bath would do me good.

CHAPTER 61

IT'S ALIVE

When Ernie rolled over, I handed him a cup of black coffee.

"It wasn't a dream, you really are here," Ernie's hangover showed in his face.

"Yep. More news, my mother is on her way here." I told him.

Ernie's eyes widened, "Your mom, why is she coming?" Ernie stood and began to *panic clean*, picking up all of his clothes from the floor.

I laughed, "What are you doing?"

Ernie's eyes went from round to bugging out, "Your mom is coming here! This place can't look like a bomb went off!" He looked at the whole trash can full of used tissue paper, "This has to be emptied, right now!" he took off outside in his boxers.

When Ernie returned from the trash, I told him, "You do know she's been on stakeout before, right? Nothing here is shocking or unexpected."

"Your mom is the best Agent I know. Not to mention, sorry Fall," Ernie put his palm up at me, "but your mom is hot!"

I shook my head and laughed.

"Do we have time to rent a carpet cleaner?" Ernie asked.

"No, we don't," I assured him. "She'll be here soon."

"Should I pick her up from the airport...I could pick her up from the airport," Ernie rambled.

"She's got all of that taken care of," I laughed.

"Should we get her flowers?" he asked seriously.

"Ernie, you're not courting my mother," I shook my head.

"It's just, she's a legend, ya know," Ernie said. "I want to make a good impression, that's all."

"Well, you've kept her son alive. I think that's the best impression she can have of you," I grinned.

"Oh, so you DID tell her about that one time?" Ernie looked hopeful.

"Yes Ernie, she knows you gave me the Heimlich maneuver during the baseball game when you thought I was choking on my hot dog."

Ernie nodded and put his hands on his hips, "It's just what I do."

I explained WHY mom was on her way to Portland, what she thought. Ernie didn't seem to question her hunch. He did, however, question what I was going to do to keep Grace safe.

"We're just going to have to keep an eye on her from a distance, like I was supposed to do in the first place," I added.

"Can't you tell her...that the threat is alive and well...and possibly in the area?"

"Right, tell her that, only after she kicked me out for finding out I was stalking her?" I questioned.

"I see your point," Ernie nodded. "You really fucked-up," he shook his head.

I nodded, "That I did. And I wouldn't give that time back for damn near anything," I admitted.

CHAPTER 62

THE GOOD, THE BAD, AND THE SECRET

Kris was no longer playing as she fastened her garter belt. Pulling up her fishnet stockings, she was prepared for whatever pain came from this. Her long bleached blonde hair was put into a ponytail, she looked in the mirror: Black merry widow that snapped at the crotch for easy access (and pushed her girls up under to damn near her chin), garter belt with fishnets, the seams running up the back of her legs, and four inch spiked black heels.

As she grabbed her purse, full of glide, lube, oils and creams, she packed in two more things...just in case. Into her overly stuffed purse went the black zip ties and a necktie. She tied her black trench coat around her and was ready to go.

Just before Kris walked out the door, her phone rang.

"Hello," she answered.

"Hi Kris, this is Jolene," came the cheery voice.

Jolene was a secretary at the precinct, and unlike the song Jolene, she was a thicker woman with blonde tightly curled hair and dimples in her round cheeks.

"Hi Jolene, I was just on my way down there," Kris said.

"Well, darn, I was hoping to catch Nate still at home," Jolene told her.

"Nate's not there?" Kris's eyes narrowed.

"Not yet, but I expect him soon. I have that report he wanted and was hoping to catch him before he left. He said it was real important, darn!" she said again.

"Hmm," Kris said. "Do me a favor, don't tell him you called...and don't tell him I'm on my way. I want to surprise my husband."

Jolene laughed, knowing full well what Kris would probably want to surprise him with. "Okay, I'll see you when you get here. Oh, he just walked in," she whispered to Kris.

"Oh good, now mum's the word, right?"

"Absolutely," Jolene assured her and giggled.

CHAPTER 63

WHAT NOW MOSCOW

"Ha!" Knushka emitted, "I kick your sorry ass!" he told Amsel, showing him his high score.

Amsel continued to pout watching Knushka enjoying his game.

A voice rang out overhead, "We will be arriving at our final destination in twenty minutes. Please fasten your seatbelts and prepare for descent.

As Knushka put down the phone to fasten his lap belt, Amsel reached for his phone.

"You touch, I break arm!" Knushka warned.

Amsel fastened his own belt then folded his arms across his chest.

As the plane touched down at a private airstrip in Eugene, Amsel looked more confused than normal, "We not in Portland?"

"We fly into Eugene. Car has been left for us to drive to Portland," Knushka informed him. "With Slovak's help, we stay *under-radar*."

As Knushka and Amsel were walked to their car both of their brows furrowed. Sitting in a tiny spot, was an even tinnier car boasting a bright green paint job.

"What this is?" Knushka's question was almost a whine as he stared at the tiny vehicular monstrosity.

"Oh, this is a *smart-car*," the young man told him.

Knushka just stared, picturing clowns jumping from the tiny automobile. "*Under-radar*, I said. What part of car…is *under-radar*? Did Slovak not communicate this to you?"

"He did," said the young Russian assistant, "but is all we have. Goes like 500 miles per charge," he added.

"Per charge?" Knushka looked confused.

"Is electric," the assistant informed him. "You have never driven electric car?"

"BMW makes electric car?" Knushka asked.

"I do not know…I think no," he shrugged.

"Then no, is answer to question," Knushka looked at the man like he was stupid.

"You will go many miles," the assistant added.

"Am not nearly so worried about miles, as I am of being seen from outer space or asked to perform at child's birthday party," Knushka informed him.

Amsel laughed hard and snorted.

"What part of this funny?" Knushka asked his nephew.

"You will look hilarious in this," Amsel blurted out without thinking.

Knushka's eyes slit.

As they pulled out of the parking lot, Knushka rode passenger in the tiny car. Amsel, being far taller than Knushka, drove with his head completely turned to one side to fit into the car. His shoulders were up against his ears as his long arms had to be contorted to move the steering wheel.

Knushka looked over at his nephew and smiled, "I look hilarious, huh…you look ridiculous."

"I cannot drive for hour with body squished this way!" he fumed.

"Oh, you know what is really sad about this?" Knushka asked.

"No," Amsel said curtly.

"Is two hours to Portland...if no traffic," Knushka laughed loudly then continued playing the *Old World Hitman* game on Amsel's phone.

CHAPTER 64

#72

As Kris again sauntered into the station, rounded eyes turned her way. Usually the looks she received were grins with a touch of longing. Today though, something in those beautiful dark eyes, made *would-be* grinners, look away.

"Where's Nate?" she asked Jolene.

The smile that never left Jolene's face, faded. "Uh, he's in the copy room."

Kris gave a grin that some would call almost sinister, not waiting to be escort by Jolene.

Sauntering into the copy room, there stood her husband reading a file. Looking up at his wife, his eyes flashed with fear.

"Hello sweetheart," she said, flat and low.

Nate closed the file and set it down, flipping the name from her view.

"What...what are you doing here, baby?" Nate stammered.

"Mmm, I woke up...I let you sleep..." she started slowly around the table that separated them. "...I made coffee...then I went to check on you."

"I...I had to leave early," he threw out the lame excuse.

"So early...you didn't even have time to kiss me goodbye." She took slow steps toward him.

"I'm so sorry about that, baby. I was so preoccupied...I feel like an asshole," he shook his head.

"Oh, I think you should," she was within three feet of him. "Because of you, I had to get dressed," she slipped off her trench coat to display her ensemble.

Nate's breath quivered as he stared at the most delicious piece of ass he had ever seen. "Baby," he shook his head, "I don't think little Nate is *up* for what you have planned."

"Really?" she closed in on her husband and began massaging little Nate. "It's funny you say that...he seems to be quite *up* for what I'm offering," she whispered in his ear.

Nate shuddered and swallowed hard, "Baby please, I'm so busy," his head fell back and his eyes closed. "And so sore," he added.

"Are you sure, baby?" she continued to rub his ridged manhood.

"What did you have in mind," he asked breathlessly.

Kris leaned back to look her husband in the eyes, "Number 72."

Nate's eyes widened, "A holier than hole-y?"

Kris grinned and slowly nodded.

Nate knew that this, number 72, was only done on special occasions and only after his wife was plied with booze. Also the stars and the moon had to be perfectly aligned, plus they had to get permission from a unicorn. This was how rarely this particular act was allowed, much less offered.

Nate was put on guard by her offer. He'd have to be, he thought. He knew she was angling for something. He knew she was trying to get the information he had promised to keep secret. But he also thought he'd have to be an idiot not to take her up on this. He pondered the situation before running to the door and clicking the lock. When he turned around she told him to sit in the chair.

"I'll guide," Kris told him.

As Nate prepared himself for number 72, Kris went into her bag of tricks. Finding the zip ties, she winked at her husband.

"You want to bind me?" he asked surprise. Not that both of them hadn't been bound at one time or another, but never at work. He preferred his hands to be free in case of the necessity for a quick re-dressing.

"Kris bit into her lower lip, "Mmhmm."

Nate loved it when she bit her lip. It meant she was thinking about what she wanted to do to him. "But then I can't hold on to your hips...I love your hips," he kissed her.

"I'll do all the work...you can have my hips later," she bit his bottom lip, then licked it seductively."

That's all it took from his lovely wife, "Okay," Nate said, putting his hands down on the armrests.

Zip tying both of his wrists, she reached for the necktie and showed it to him.

Concern flashed across Nate's face as he started to say, "Wait a min..."

That's as far as he got before Kris shoved the tie in his mouth.

Nate's brow furrowed as he watched her pick up the file on the table. Showing him the name on the file, her eyes flashed with pure rage.

Kris asked, "Why didn't you say anything?"

Nate tried to speak through the tie, but wasn't making sense.

Kris said, "I'm going to give you one chance to tell me everything. If I feel like you aren't being 100% honest with me, I will leave you bound; gagged and little Nate will make his first police station debut. Do we understand each other?"

Nate nodded to his wife, realizing that he had made a serious faux pas in judgment.

Removing the gag, she asked, "What is Grace caught up in?"

"Well, I don't know a whole lot, but..."

Kris picked up the tie and turned half crazed eyes on her husband.

"Okay, that guy that's staying at her house...the one you had me run a background check on..."

"Yeah?" Kris's fear was showing.

"He's an FBI agent. It seems that he's working on a case that involves one of Grace's neighbors."

"What kind of case? Does Grace know he's FBI?"

"He only told me what he could, it's an open case," Nate shook his head.

"He TOLD YOU?" Kris wanted to know. "When?"

"The other day...the mystery phone call. He said he was staying at Gracie's to protect her. He asked me not to tell you because he knew you'd go there...get in the middle of things and put yourself in danger. He said it was easier if all he had to worry about was Grace. But he swore he would protect her with his life. So I looked him up and he's a straight shooter...a great agent. She's safer with him than anyone, or I would have gone myself to protect her."

"Why didn't he just send her home...to us?" Kris asked.

Nate didn't want to answer this part, "The guy...the one the Agent is trying to bring down...he's kind of known, for not letting anyone who could rat him out...live. Fall didn't want the guy to come looking for her here...at her parents house."

Kris's eyes rounded, "Are you fuckin' kidding me? How could you keep this from me?"

"Because...you can't keep her safe Kris," her husband told her.

With that, her eyes flashed, hot. Kris grabbed her purse and stormed out leaving Nate bound to a chair, with his member peeking out of his pants.

Three seconds later, Kris walked back in and Nate started to thank her, but then she gagged him again and tucked little Nate away.

"Mmmm mmm mmm mmmmm?" Nate muffled to his wife.

"Me? I'm going to Gracie's," she took his gun out of his holster and slipped it in her trench coat pocket.

Nate's eyes went wide, seeing his wife armed.

"And I put little Nate away only because of that young new recruit you told me about that stares at you in the shower. I'm not having him picturing you 72-ing him all over the place. And just so you know, if anything happens to Gracie, you won't have anything to *#72 with*!" she slammed the door behind her.

Nate knew this was true.

In the car, Kris tried to call Grace, but got no answer. She debated leaving a message, but what if the bad guy was there? She didn't want to put anyone on alert. Especially Grace. She wasn't good under pressure, she assessed as she pulled away from the station, tires screeching.

CHAPTER 65

HUMILIATION SERVED COLD

As much as Nate didn't want anyone to find him this way, the fear of his wife running full bore into danger, would *void* any embarrassment he may have felt.

Pushing the tie from his mouth took some work. Once he could speak, he called out, "I need a little help in here," hoping someone would hear him. "A little help," he yelled louder.

Just then, in walked the new recruit...the one who often stole glances at Nate's manhood in the shower at the department gym.

"I heard you calling," he said coming through the door. "Oh my," he said seeing Nate's predicament, his eyes appreciating the view. "What happened to you?" the recruit's hand fluttered to his chest.

Nate rolled his eyes, "Can you please just get me loose?"

"Righty-o," the young officer told him.

"Maybe we could keep this between us?" Nate asked. "I really don't need this passed around the office."

"Absolutely, I'm really good at keeping secrets," he winked.

Nate let out a sigh, "Great."

Running out to his Bronco, Nate noticed that his tires had been flattened...by a knife. "Yep, she's pissed," he said to no one.

Nate ran back inside to the Chief of Police, "Uncle Mac, I need your car. Kris popped my tires."

"I'm not dumb enough to give you my vehicle when your wife's pissed, son," his Uncle Mac told him.

"Did I mention she has my gun?" Nate whispered.

Uncle Mac handed him the keys, "There's a flak jacket in the trunk. God speed!"

CHAPTER 66

GRACE GOES FULL GRACIE

I started with the baseboards. This is what I did when I was stressed. Once the baseboards were sparkling, I tackled the shower tiles. Putting on my yellow rubber gloves, I heard the phone ring. Walking into the kitchen, I just stared at it. Picking up the receiver, I saw Kris's name on the screen. I knew now that I wouldn't be able to vent to her, to explain anything without God-knows-who listening. I let it ring and grabbed my cell. Dialing Kris's number, it went straight to voicemail. I left her a message saying that if she wanted to contact me, it would have to be on my cell. No reason, no explanation, just call me back, please. Back into the bathroom I headed to re-scrub my already clean tub.

CHAPTER 67

THE MOTHER OF ALL MOTHERS

When Anya's plane landed, there was indeed a government vehicle waiting for her. Anya smirked, she knew her man very well. Even from a far, he was always looking out for her. The last twenty-five years with Agent Barnes had been wonderful. And even though she refused to marry him, it wasn't for his *lacking* in any way.

Getting into the backseat of the blacked out Chevy Suburban, she pulled out her cell.

"Agent Barnes," she said when he answered the phone.

"So you've made it safely to Portland, I see."

She knew she was on his radar 24/7. "And comfortably, I might add. Thank you very much."

"Well, I know how you love your personal space," he grinned.

He was well aware of the fact than Anya was in fact a lover of her personal space. Only two men in her life were allowed to penetrate her bubble of comfort. Agent Barnes was proud to be one of them.

"You know me so very well," she laughed.

"Our dog misses you," Agent Barnes informed her. "Our bed misses you."

"And you?" Anya asked coyly.

Agent Barnes let out a sigh, "Every moment you are away...is just a small slice of hell for me."

Anya knew this was true, because she felt the same way.

"I love you, Anya," Barnes told her.

"I would mourn you if you died," she told him.

When she hung up the phone, she felt the tugging of her heart strings. The truth was Barnes had been such an amazing part of her life. As an Agent, she always had both feet set firmly on the ground. Her life was steeped in reality, all things that were palpable; proof, evidence that could be verified; everything had to be tangible or clearly visible. Speculation was only used to gain more access so one could continue searching for the palpable and tangible.

Ah, but love she thought, you can have proof; the things they do, the way they act, the things they say, and unfortunately, even with all this evidence, you can still be wrong.

She remembered how leery she was of Agent Barnes's intentions when they first started dating. Anya had grown cold from a past mistreating. She swore to herself she would never again let love abuse her so. Yet, her attraction to Barnes was present. She fought the feeling at every turn, insisting that they remain professional. Then one serendipitous day...an investigation took a turn for the worse.

Shots flew and Anya was hit in the shoulder. Under heavy fire of semi-automatic weapons, Barnes threw her over his shoulder and proceeded to run her to safety. When she asked him why he would do something so stupid, so ill-thought-out, (deciding then that if his reasoning had anything to do with her being a woman, she would beat his ass), "Because I would mourn if you died," he said, fearful of expressing his true feelings. Finally, working up all the courage he had, he said, "I love you. I have since the first day I laid eyes on you. And some part of me...wasn't sure I could live without you. And EVERY part of me...doesn't want to."

Anya grew a little misty thinking of this moment, this cherished memory. I guess it had had something to do with me being a woman, she thought and grinned. But, that memory had kept her from killing him through the numerous fights and squabbles that all couples have. She would remember this moment, and her anger, no matter how well deserved, faded into nothingness.

Looking out the window she noticed that highway 205 was backed up as far as the eye could see. Sitting back in her seat, she decided to relax for a moment. If her intuition was correct, this may very well be her last chance to do this for awhile.

CHAPTER 68

TOUCH DOWN

"Mom's plane is on the ground," I told Ernie, who had been cleaning since he heard she was coming.

I couldn't really blame him. My mother was indeed a legend in the Bureau. She had more busts and arrests under her belt, save for her previous partner, who was now SSA, Barnes.

I had never met the man until I was eight years old (even though she worked with him for the three years prior to our meeting). She had been shot during a surveillance detail. I remembered walking into her hospital room and seeing this man sitting next to her bed. Although she was unconscious, he held her hand. As I stepped in, he turned his attention to me. Tears streamed down his cheeks. I knew two things right then; this man...loved my mother. And, I would be an agent someday.

Just then the phone tap clicked on, drawing me away from my memory. I waited for Grace to answer. When she didn't, I checked the machine to see where the call had come from. It was Kris. As the machine clicked off, I couldn't help but wonder...why wouldn't her best friend leave a message? I could guess why Grace wasn't answering, but if Kris knew what was going on, she wouldn't leave a message, would she?

Ernie answered the phone in the room when it rang. It was our call center saying they had taken a message for me. Taking the phone, I knew mom would have called my cell.

"Agent Linn here, you have a message for me?" I asked.

"Yes. A male; first name Nate, identified himself as an officer in a small town 42 miles east of you says; 'She knows and she's on her way'. He went on to say that she's armed. Should we send out more units?"

I shook my head, "No, we're fine. Thank you."

I was going to meet the infamous Kris, I thought as I hung up the phone. I let Ernie know that soon, we would have company.

Ernie began undressing, as my face squished up, "What are you doing?" I asked.

Grabbing his flak jacket he said, "I'm more afraid of that crazy bitch than I am Knushka."

Going over in my head all the things Grace had told me about Kris, I had to agree.

CHAPTER 69

ZZZZZZZZZZZZZ

Getting close to Portland, Knushka's nerves were fraying; partly because of his inability to pass the level on the hitman game he was playing. And partly because of the *zzzz-ing* sound the tiny car made. He felt like a hamster on a wheel.

Amsel still drove with his head cocked over to one shoulder and arms crunched up. His legs had to be spread wide so that his knees didn't impede the movement of the steering wheel.

Seeing this, made Knushka smile. Even though he didn't get to neutralize his giant pain in the ass, he did get to torture him.

"How much further we go?" Amsel asked.

"Until we get there," Knushka offered.

"How many more miles?" Amsel rephrased his question.

Knushka looked at the sign they were passing, "30 miles, we be there."

Amsel let out a heavy sigh, but didn't dare complain.

CHAPTER 70

KRIS TO THE RESCUE

One bar, no bar, one bar, no bar, "Dammit," Kris yelled at her phone.

Driving through the mountains was beautiful...unless you needed dependable cell coverage. She was aware that she was driving too fast for some of these curves especially after a heavy snow fall. Slowing down a bit, she began to offer deals to God.

"If you make sure that Grace is okay, and I mean 100% okay, I will..." Kris furrowed her brow. She didn't know what to offer. She already went to church...sometimes. She donated time and money to several organizations. She knew that you didn't make unrealistic deals with God. I mean, I'm not going to go to the North Pole to feed Polar Bears, she thought. What did she have to barter with that was hard to do, almost impossible, but yet still possible? Kris took a deep breath as she settled on her deal.

"If you save Grace from any and all danger, I'll give up sex, in all forms, for a month," she said out loud, (Which, to her knowledge, was the only way to make her deal with God, legal.) After saying it, she felt sick to her stomach. She knew she could have just said she wouldn't do #72. But given her very rare desire to 72, she knew God wouldn't consider her sacrifice worthy of much.

"Twenty more miles of winding road," she tried to steady her breathing.

CHAPTER 71

MAMA, I'M COMING HOME

As I scrubbed the baseboards and shower tiles until it sparkled, I shook my head.

"What are you doing, Grace?" I asked no one.

Heading into the bedroom, I pulled my suitcase out of the closet. It used to be, the thought of going back to the small town I grew up in was torture. Now, the thought of being here in my own apartment was too much to bear! I shook my head. It would do me good to go home for the remainder of my vacation. Seeing my mom and dad, and Kris...this would be good therapy for me. Packing some warm clothes, sox, toothbrush and gloves, I zipped the case closed.

After another cup of coffee, I would head out, giving the icy roads home a little time to thaw. I pushed *PLAY* on my CD player and walked to my couch. Otis began to sing. I made it halfway through *I've Been Loving You Too Long,* then walked over and turned off my stereo.

"Fuck the roads, I'm outta here!" I grabbed my purse, coat and suitcase then headed out the door.

Walking to my POS car, a tiny neon green car pulled up in

front of me, blocking my path. I don't know what I expected to pop out of that tiny car; but who did, scared the hell out of me.

CHAPTER 72

WHAT THE HELL

Kris was almost there, two more lights. She dialed Grace again. Again the message played as Kris drove on. When the message beeped, Kris was right in front of the apartment building waiting for the light that would allow her to turn left into the complex.

"Grace, I'm here. I wanted to tell you I was coming, but I didn't want to alarm you, but now...what the hell?" she said into the machine. "Now I'm watching you being shoved into a bright green smart car. Oh hell no! Grace, Grace!" she screamed out the window. Dropping the phone, Kris made an illegal turn right in front of oncoming traffic, almost causing a collision. Her Bronco was now chasing the tiny green car. She passed a tall man that she had seen discarded from the car before it pulled away. He acted like he was going to try and block her, but Kris never slowed down. The tall thin man with shoulder length dark hair and his neck kinked to the left, jumped out of her way as she sped through the parking lot.

CHAPTER 73

SECRETS AND TRUTHS

As I stood frozen by fear in my parking lot, "Oh shit," escaped my mouth as Knushka exited the tiny car in front of me. Showing me the gun on his hip, he asked where the package was.

"I don't have it," I stammered, shaking my head,

"Where it goes?" Knushka asked.

I couldn't tell him about Fall, that they were *onto* him...watching. "I never got a package," my head shook again. I wasn't sure he believed me.

Just then, I heard Kris yelling to me, "Grace, Grace?" Hanging out of her Bronco, she screamed.

"You get in car," Knushka said, "or I turn you...and her," his head cocked to where Kris was getting ready to turn, "into Swiss's cheeses."

I got into the passenger seat. The guy who had been the driver asked, "Where I sit?" since there was definitely no back seat in this thing.

Knushka told him to find a way back to the airport in Eugene, or find a job, "Either way...not my problem."

Over my shoulder, I could see Krissy's Bronco coming quickly through the lot. Before I could turn my head back around, I felt a pinprick.

"Oh my God! Oh my God! Oh my God!" I panicked as Knushka shot something into my vein. "Am I gonna die now?" I asked as the little car zipped away.

"No, no, not yet," Knushka said. "I have questions, so I gave you shot of Sodium Pentothal mixed with amnesia drug being tested in Russia. My own mix," he said with pride, "is very effective and longer lasting."

Within moments, my vision blurred and my panic breathing slowed to calm. A tiny smile pulled up both of my cheeks.

"There it is," he said to me. "Who is in Bronco following us?"

I laughed, "That's my best friend, Krissy."

"She is police?"

"No...but her husband Nate is," I nodded.

"Hmm, did you receive package?" he asked.

"Mmm," I laughed, then pursed my lips and shook my head.

"You did NOT receive package, then?" he questioned.

I kept my lips pursed and tried not to laugh, as we *zzzzz'd* away.

"You answer me!" Knushka demanded.

The look on his face, made me snort. "You answer me!" I mocked in my best Russian accent. "You have...kind of a Moose and Squirrel thing, going on," my head bobbed back and forth. "It's kind of...sexy in a Boris and Natasha way..." I blinked hard.

CHAPTER 74

OH SHIT....OH SHIT

Oh shit, was Fall's first thought when he heard Kris on Grace's machine. She was here. But then Kris said that a man in a green smart car had abducted Grace. He heard wheels screeching and looked out the window. A neon green smart car wound through the internal complex below with a Bronco right behind it.

"Shit Ernie, let's go!" Fall yelled.

The '68 Charger fired up and burned out of the parking lot in hot pursuit.

CHAPTER 75

RULES ARE MEANT TO BE BROKEN

Agent Anya Linn answered her son's call.

"Where are you mom?" he asked. She could hear the panic in his voice.

"One mile before the Sunnyside exit," she told him.

"Don't get off the freeway yet. Grace has been abducted by someone in a neon green smart car."

Anya furrowed her brow at the thought of a smart-car abduction.

"We're in pursuit...okay...he's waiting for a chance to get on the 205 heading South."

"I'm right behind you, son," Anya told him. "Pull over," she said to the agent who had been assigned as her driver.

"Excuse me, ma'am," he said.

"Please don't make me repeat myself," the look on her face giving ample warning.

Within two shakes of a lamb's tail, Anya pulled the suburban across three lanes of traffic and sped to assist her son. Attaching a police light to the top of the vehicle, Portland drivers quickly moved out of her way.

"Ma'am," said the young agent, "should I be worried...about

breaking the rules?" his eyes were round with fright.

Anya grinned at him, "You have heard of me?" she asked him.

Under his breath he said, "Oh shit."

Anya grinned, "Call the department and let them know that there's been an abduction of one of our witnesses. Case file name: RussiaOR225. Dmitri Knushka is most likely the suspect. Undoubtedly he is armed and very dangerous."

"Yes ma'am, anything else?" the young agent asked.

"Let them know that agents Anya Linn and Fall Linn are in pursuit. Give them our location and have them send out an APB. Instruct them NOT to interfere as of right now. The car we're chasing...can't go faster than the speed limit."

"Mom, mom," Anya could hear coming from her phone.

"I'm here son, any idea where we're heading? Does he have property here?"

"No, and I can't imagine where he's planning on going on the 205 South. Soon we'll be out of the city and in the country."

Anya looked at her young passenger, "I need a list of all airports, commercial and private down the 205 South," she told him.

"Do you really think he's going to an airport?" Fall asked.

"He had to fly into Portland somehow. Unless he showed up in a very good disguise, his movements would have been tracked from any commercial airport he left from or landed in," his mother told him. "By the way, why won't that Bronco get out of the way?" Anya could see that the little green car was followed closely by a Bronco.

"That's Grace's best friend. She doesn't really know what's going on, but she witnessed the abduction."

"Does she know she's in danger?" Anya questioned.

"I really don't think she cares," Fall told his mother. "Plus, she's armed according to her husband...a police officer."

Anya grinned, "I like her already."

CHAPTER 76

SON OF A...

Nate pulled up in front of Grace's apartment. Her car was there, but Kris's Bronco wasn't. He wondered if maybe they went to breakfast. A tall thin man with a crick in his neck sat on a parking curb, his hands holding up his crooked head.

"You didn't see a Bronco go through here, did you?" Nate asked.

The man's eyes bugged out of his skull. He said something in Russian before standing quickly and trying to run. Running, with his head cocked to one side made equilibrium almost impossible. Nate was on him within moments and had him cuffed.

CHAPTER 77

REALLY?

"Is sexy?" I asked.

"Sure," Grace said. "You know my friend, Krissy...the one following us?" She pointed her thumb to indicate the Bronco behind us. "Kris and her husband...do ummm...I think it's number 18, and...and he does it...with an accent like yours," she pointed to me and grinned.

Knushka's bushy brows arched, "Does what...exactly?"

"Well, I can't say...EXACTLY, but I know it's one of their *sex numbers*," Grace whispered the last part.

"Sex numbers?" I asked. "What this is, sex numbers?"

Grace cleared her throat, "It's like this..." she began.

Knushka listened intently as Grace explained several different sex numbers; what they entailed, props used and which ones could be asked for, depending on the level of *angry*.

Certain numbers were for small things like scratching the car or forgetting to mail-off the power bill. Other numbers were for bigger offenses, like a car accident or the power being shut off. There were a few sex numbers that were so taboo, Grace couldn't even imagine what atrocities had to be committed to even be allowed to request them, but they were there none the less.

Grace looked behind her at Krissy's Bronco still right on the tiny car's tail. She began to laugh, "I bet this one will cost her a #72," she shook her head and laughed hysterically.

"What is #72," I looked sidelong at Grace, with questioning.

CHAPTER 78

SOMEONE TO WATCH OVER ME

Anya's cell phone rang and she put the call on speaker.

"So you've been there what...forty-five minutes?" Agent Barnes's voice rang loud and clear.

Anya grinned. She knew that as soon as the young Agent sitting in the passenger seat sent out the APB, she could expect a call.

"I'm sorry Agent Barnes," she grinned, "are you implying that this fiasco somehow surrounds me?"

"I'm sorry, implying this was unfair. I should have just stated it as a matter of fact," he said.

Anya could almost see his grin. He knew better than anyone how badly she wanted to be the one to take Knushka down.

"I take it the woman who was abducted is Fall's heartthrob?"

"Indeed," Anya confirmed.

"How is my boy handling it?" Agent Barnes asked.

"Much like you did," Anya informed him.

Barnes let out a heavy sigh, "Poor kid. He must be a damn wreck."

"Absolutely," Anya said.

"We've got eyes," Agent Barnes told his love.

"I expected nothing less."

CHAPTER 79

YOU'VE GOTTA BE KIDDING ME

"Shit," Fall said.

"I really don't want to hear that right now," Ernie told him.

"I didn't fill the fucking tank. If he goes much further, we're going to run out of gas."

"Are you kidding?" Ernie spat. "What are you, a fuckin' rookie?"

"You can chastise me later. I need you to get my mom on the phone. Tell her what's happening and to pick us up!"

As they pulled over, Anya was five seconds behind. Piling into the backseat of the Suburban, they were off again.

"You're lucky they're driving that clown car," Anya told her son. "Otherwise we'd never catch back up!" She sped away and pushed the gas pedal to the floor.

"I know, I know, I fucked up!" I told her. "Just please, don't let anything happen to her!"

Anya's eyes found her son's in the rearview mirror. He wasn't the cool, calm man she had always known him to be. This was no crush. This wasn't adrenaline. This was what a man in love looked like, acted like, when his love was threatened.

CHAPTER 80

OMG

Knushka nodded his head, but took a moment to respond. "Yes very few women ask for #72," he agreed. "Even fewer appreciate a SLIP," he confirmed and made finger quotes.

There was a moment of silence where Knushka and Grace just nodded some more.

"But sounds like friend..."

"Kris," Grace offered with a slightly drunken and off-kilter smile.

"Right...Kris and husband, have found good way to work through marital problems," Knushka admitted. "I mean, always *making love* from *anger*...not a bad way to do it."

Grace's phone rang and she dug for it in her purse. "It's Kris!" she showed Knushka the name.

"You answer? I would like to hear voice of this woman," Knushka said "I bet is sexy."

"Okie-dokey," Grace told him. "Hello," Grace said into the receiver.

"Put her on speaker," Knushka whispered.

CHAPTER 81

GRACE???

"Hello," I said to my best friend in the whole wide world.

"What the fuck is going on?" Kris yelled.

Knushka and I both shot our heads back and stared at the yelling phone.

"Maybe not voice right now is sexy?" Knushka said under his breath.

"Don't yell, I hate it when you yell," I pouted.

"Grace, are you...drunk?" Kris asked.

"No...my friend Knushkasss, gave me a...a...shot! Some kind of serum, which by the way, he invented himself," I gave Knushka a smile and a nod. "I think I may need more," I told him.

"GRACE!" Kris yelled, "ARE YOU OKAY?"

"Oh yeah, Knushy and I are just talking...about...well, YOU!" I began to laugh.

"Me? What about me? What are you telling him about me," Kris demanded.

"About your sex," I whispered.

"WHAT?" Kris sounded angry.

"Don't be mad, he say's you and Nate have a really good approach to marital anger," I let her know.

"Yes, is really very good. Much better than how I handled anger with wife," Knushka admitted.

"Oh, did you two have a fight?" I asked sympathetically.

"No," Knushka shook his head, "I kill her!" he admitted.

My eyes rounded.

"YOU KILLED YOUR WIFE?" Kris screamed, horrified.

"Well, yes, but was when I was young. I had much to work through, so much anger," his head shook. "And psychiatrist said that overbearing mother and absent father, had something to do with problems, was a lot of therapy needed."

I nodded like I understood, patting Knushka's shoulder. "You grew up without a dad?" I was on the verge of tears. "Did he abandon you and you mother?"

"No, he dies in line of duty," Knushka said proudly.

"Oh, he was military?" I asked.

"No, he was mob boss. Shot seventeen times in back."

"Oh," was all I had.

"Ah, Nudgey, or whatever the hell your name is, WHY WOULD YOU KILL YOUR WIFE?" Kris demanded to know just what kind of a sick-o had taken me hostage.

"Well, she was having...you know...with someone else," he explained.

"Well now you're in my wheelhouse," I nodded.

"You were cheated? Pretty girl like you?" Knushka looked skeptical. "No!"

"Oh yes sir," my head bobbled. "Walked in on him...screwing that *she-bat* of a mistress on my kitchen table. I loved that kitchen table," I added.

"Is awful," Knushka's head shook. "You give me address, and I have them both taken care of. Or just one of them. Your choice. I know how bad must be for you...seeing these things."

"It was pretty bad," I agreed. "Probably the worst thing I've ever seen," I said.

"I walked in on wife, too."

"No," I shook my head.

"She was boffing brother," he explained.

"Oh my God...how do you even decide which one betrayed you the worst? I mean really?" I patted him again.

"Is why I killed them both," Knushka shrugged. "Cannot hold one responsible and not other...is unfair!"

"Right?" I agreed.

"Not right," Kris busted in on the truly strange bonding moment Knushy and I were having. "Killing is not right, EVER!" Kris informed us. "And if one fucking hair on Grace's head is harmed, I will rip your fucking throat out, shit down your neck and use your tongue to wipe my ass, before I send you down a slide of razorblades into a pool of FUCKING ACID," she yelled.

Knushka eyes popped, "She would have been great on payroll."

"I think she's still mad about the sex stuff I told you," I whispered to him.

"I'm not mad about that Grace!" Kris yelled again.

My head bobbed up and down, "I didn't tell him about the book?" I shook my head at the receiver.

"Book, she writes book...about sex?" Knushka's eyes showed interest. "What...what is in book she writes?"

CHAPTER 82

JOIN THE PARTY

Looking behind us, all you could see for miles was a slew of police cars, motorcycle officers, and SUV's.

"The good part is, there's no chance he'll get away," Anya told her son.

"Yeah, but the bad part is, he has nothing to lose by killing Grace," I told my mother. "She can prove how many packages have been delivered to her. We only KNOW of two and still can't pin them on him. She can."

I had never been this worried before in all of my life. My palms were sweating and I couldn't stop making up scenarios in my head that I didn't want to come true. There was nothing I wouldn't have done to keep her safe, even if it meant my job. And just look at what kind of fuck-up I allowed to happen to her.

CHAPTER 83

IN HOT PURSUIT

"Ma'am, I have information on all the airports between here and Medford," said the rookie agent. "But there is only one that had an international flight logged for last night. It came from Russia, he told Anya.

Anya asked, "What airport?"

"Eugene," he told her and gave her the address.

We were still an hour away from Eugene, and we didn't dare move in. The more pressure Knushka felt, the more likely he would be to take drastic measures.

Anya knew her son well. A normal mother would have offered some kind of soothing words. How she longed to be able to do this for him now. But Anya knew full well how he had been trained, and by who. She knew that right now his mind was rolling over all of the possible scenarios, assessing the damage, both departmental and collateral. She also knew that this Grace Fully, whoever she was, meant something to him. If she didn't, he would never have broken protocol. Not the stickler he was. She, herself, had broken the rules a few times and had paid whatever consequences were demanded for her choices. She just hoped his wouldn't be a broken heart...or worse.

CHAPTER 84

BONDING WITH GRACE

Knushka had to admit, he was having a good time. He barely even heard the sirens behind him as he and Grace made small talk.

"So, what is in book that friend...," Knushka was cut off.

"Kris," Grace's head bobbed.

"Kris," Knushka repeated, "what she writes about?"

"Well...it's kind of like a ...rule book for women," Grace told him.

"Rules...rules of sex?" Knushka looked confused.

"More like rules of relationships. The *must do's*," Grace's eyes widened.

Knushka was pretty sure what that entailed.

"And the things you should never do," Grace shook her head.

"Like #72?" Knushka wanted to know.

Grace's head shook some more, "No, no...that's discretionary. Totally a case by case basis," she put up her palm. "What I'm talking about is like...*why you never wear red underwear*."

Knushka's eyes shot to Grace, who sat nodding at nothing. "Why no red? I love red!" Knushka informed her.

"No, see, you can wear red...just not the *first time* you're with a man, at least, not if you like him, like him."

"I do not understand," his bushy brows met in the middle of his forehead.

"See," Grace began explaining, "If a woman wears black, white, pink..."

Knushka cut her off, "Yellow?"

"Ew, who looks good in yellow?" Grace posed the question.

Knushka's smile stretched across his face, "Latina women."

"You know what," Grace agreed, "I have to give you that one. I mean Sofia Vergara, WOW. I bet she looks great in yellow!"

"Ah yes, the Modern Family woman," Knushka's head bobbed up and down, "she is WOW. But back too red...what is wrong with red?"

"Well, if a woman wears ANY other color...ya know...your first time, it's a good sign."

"Yes, okay, but why is red wrong first time," Knushka prodded.

"If she wears red the first time you're together, it means she's a slut, and will most likely cheat on you," Grace said.

There was silence while Knushka tried to figure this out. "Only when she wears for first time?" he lifted one brow.

"Yeah, if she wears red after the first time...then she's still a slut...but she's YOUR slut. If she wears it the first time...she's EVERYONE'S slut," Grace said dramatically.

Knushka thought about this and let out a, "Hmm."

"It's not scientific," Grace shrugged, "just an observation."

Knushka was nodding, "Wife wore red first time. Think maybe your friend..."

"Kris," Grace smiled.

"...think she may be onto something," Knushka offered.

"You hear that, Kris," Grace said into her phone. "Hello? Kriiiiisss?" she called out, with no reply.

CHAPTER 85

MAKING UP...

Kris had just plugged in her charger when her phone started to ring. Looking at the display, her eyes slit.

"Oh, I can't wait to hear this," is how she answered.

"Honey look, I know you're pissed, but I was trying to protect not just you and Grace's whole family, but Grace as well!" Nate told her. "You have to know that!"

Kris was bull-breathing through her nostrils, "Do you have any idea what kind of madman has Grace? HE KILLED HIS WIFE!"

"Oh God," Nate expelled.

"That's not even the freakiest part...he and Grace are...like bonding over OUR sex-life!"

Nate fell silent.

"Did you hear me?" Kris asked.

"Uh, yeah," Nate said slowly.

"You don't think that's weird?" she questioned her husband.

"No, of course I do, it just...our sex life is kind of...incredible, ya know?"

She had no haughty retort to this. He was her *Well-Endowed-Engine-Who-Could* and *Did*, and she was his *conductor*.

"Did I mention he drugged her?" Kris was on the verge of

angry tears. "And now, she's calling him *Knushers* or something like that. She's so out of it! AND WHERE THE FUCK ARE THEY GOING? We've been on this freeway for like an hour now."

"That's one of the things I can tell you!" Nate told his wife. Nate explained how he had come after her.

"I was just a few minutes behind you. I asked some guy sitting out in front of Grace's apartment if he had seen your Bronco," he began.

"I wonder if that's the guy I almost ran over?" Kris said more to herself than to her husband.

Nate was silent while he pondered what his wife was willing to do to save Grace.

"Long story short, I apprehended the guy. He's Knushka's accomplice...and he's not very bright," Nate whispered into the phone. "Anyway, he told me that Knushka is heading to a small airport in Eugene. You said you've been on the road for almost an hour? That should put you at right around the Salem area."

"We're about ten miles out," Kris confirmed.

"Do they have a whole slew of officers following you?" Nate asked his wife.

"They're holding back, but yes about ten cars. There's a Suburban on my ass with a flashing light on the hood," Kris confirmed.

"Why haven't you moved out of their way?" Nate sounded shocked.

Kris stayed silent.

"Right, please be careful. This guy is really dangerous," he said, knowing he just answered his own question. "The police are coming to pick up this guy I have in custody," Nate looked over at Amsel. "I love you, Kris."

Again there was silence.

"You're not going to say you love me, too?"

"Let's see how this plays out," she answered, knowing full well that she was now worried for her husband's safety as well as Grace's. What if this psycho he had detained was an escape artist or Kung Fu master? Now she knew why her husband hadn't told her. Her mind would go off the deep end sometimes when it came to the people she loved most.

Finally, she said, "I love you, too, Nate. Please be careful."

CHAPTER 86

INFORMATION SHARING

Fall dialed the number he had called Nate at a couple of days earlier.

"Is this your wife we're following?" Fall asked.

"Yes it is and no...she won't be getting out of your way," Nate told him."

Fall cracked a small smile and shook his head. "What can we expect from her?"

"Well, she armed, there's that."

"She carries?" Fall asked.

"No, I carry...and because of that, she's now carrying," Nate informed him.

"She took your gun?" Fall's eyes rounded.

"Yes...yes she did."

"Do we have anything to worry about? I mean is she a good shot at least?" Fall looked worried and saw more scenarios beginning to flash in his head.

"A crack shot," Nate told him. "She placed expert."

"She's an officer?" Fall was confused by this.

"Nope, she just got the chief to allow her to compete in the PPC for the department. He offered her a job afterward."

Again, Fall grinned. "She's not always logical when it comes to people she loves, though, right?"

"Actually, she's incredibly logical...she runs over every scenario in her head, then tries to manipulate the situation to follow the best possible outcome. She may go into action on a whim, but believe me, she's thinking of everything that could go wrong...and how to make it right." Nate explained.

Fall's brows lifted, "Sounds like she would have made a great Agent."

Nate agreed. "I have Knushka's accomplice. He said that they were supposed to head to an airport in Eugene."

"We're headed that way now," Fall told him. "I'll have someone from the department pick up Knushka's accomplice."

"Keep my wife safe," Nate said.

"I intend to," Fall told him.

CHAPTER 87

YOU AND YOUR EXPLANATIONS

Grace's phone rang again. Thinking Kris was calling back, Grace answered it with "I told Knushy about #72," she laughed.

"What?" I asked her. "Grace, it's Fall, are you okay?"

"Oh, it's you," she said. "Yeah, I'm fine. Knushy and I are just getting to know each other."

"Grace, he's a very dangerous man," I told her, when I heard Knushka say, "Put on speaker."

"Okay," Grace giggled.

"Who is on phone?" Knushka's voice rang out.

"Agent Linn, FBI," I answered.

"Any relation to Agent Anya Linn?" Knushka wanted to know.

I looked at my mother, and she nodded. "Yes. I'm her son."

"Oh, is family affair, being Agent. How is mother?" he asked.

"She's well. Actually, she's driving the Suburban two cars behind you," I informed him.

"Always I liked your mother, beautiful woman, if not a little obsessive about me. Maybe she had crush?" Knushka wondered out loud.

Mom grinned, "Hello Knushka."

"So nice to hear voice. Have you missed me?" Knushka asked her.

"So far, every time," Mom admitted.

Knushka laughed. "I can't believe your son called to talk to me. Not with beautiful woman sitting beside me, he appears to know by name."

"You're right," I told him. "Grace? Are you alright?" I repeated.

"I'm good. We're just driving. Nice day for a drive," Grace said.

"I need you to know that I'm going to do everything to make sure you're safe."

"Oh, that's sweet," Grace told him.

"You ARE in danger," I said, hoping some of this would get through her haze.

"What danger, I'm with Knushy!" she expelled. "We're bonding!"

"Well, Knushy is a criminal. He's not a good guy." I couldn't very well let her know that the reason he took her was to use her to barter his situation, or worse.

"I don't know why you care," she said clearly. "I mean, I'm just some girl that got caught up in an investigation. Just some girl whose phone you tapped."

"You tap phone," Knushka piped up. "Is nothing sacred anymore?"

"Look can I say something?" I asked.

"Sure," Knushka told him.

"Not to you...to her," I clarified.

"Oh, she is nodding, go ahead," Knushka said.

"I tapped your phone...not because of the investigation. I tapped your phone," I let out a deep sigh, "because...because...I would mourn you if you died."

Anya's head turned to her son.

CHAPTER 88

HUH???

"You would MOURN ME, if I died?" I asked him.

Knushka gave a shrug of his shoulders, "I know not how to take this."

"Neither do I," I slurred a little. "That's morbid. I mean, thanks, but damn!" I said into the phone. "Ya know, it's weird, I am sooo bad at reading things. I...I thought we had, like, a moment. I...I...REALLY did. Do you know I shaved my legs?"

"You no keep them shaved?" Knushka asked.

"Oh please," my head turned to Knushka. "It's winter...in Portland, and I haven't been touched in over a year. Why the hell would I shave?" I asked. "I'll tell you why, because I thought something was happening between us," I told Fall. "But then again, I was also the girl who thought she was happily married, so what does that tell you?"

"Something was...happening," Fall said back. "Something I thought was...inappropriate...to share."

"Inappropriate? What the hell does that even mean?" I asked Knushy like he would know. "What does that mean?" I yelled into the receiver.

"Uh...well...uh," Fall stammered.

Ernie stared at Fall, then his face squished up, "Ah man!"

A grin pulled up one side of Knushka's face, "I think I know what inappropriate was," he began laughing.

"You stay out of this," Fall warned him.

"What, she is beautiful girl!" Knushka laughed at him. "I could see this causing INAPPROPIATENESS," Knushka hit the word hard.

"You let me make an ASS out of myself," I said. "I almost kissed you!"

"What is light flashing on dash?" Knushka asked me, as I hung up the phone.

CHAPTER 89

IS NO GOOD

"Light blinks on dash, what this means?" Knushka looked at Grace.

"Um," she squinted at the dashboard. "I think that means...your charge is running low? It's like a little plug symbol or something."

"Stupid electric car! Will run five-hundred miles, my tookus!" Knushka fumed.

"Maybe there's someplace we can charge it?" Grace offered.

She really wasn't grasping the situation, Knushka thought. "I do not think is in officer's plans to let this happen."

"Maybe you could call a timeout?" Grace's eyes went wide with question.

Knushka's lips pursed, "Going to have to use plan B."

"Oh, what's plan B?" Grace smiled.

"I haven't thought of it yet," Knushka moved out of the fast lane to the slow lane.

"Hey, we're in Salem!" Grace clapped. "I love Salem."

CHAPTER 90

YET ANOTHER PERSPECTIVE

Out on a little dirt road just outside of Salem, a band of officers gathered and were briefed about the raid.

Detective Owens updated his men.

"We'll have eight going through the front door, and another eight officers going through the back. We'll go on three. This is their meeting time, so we're more likely to grab the lot of them. Remember they are armed and possibly dangerous," he gave a palms-up, "no matter what you think when you see them," Detective Owens informed his men with a headshake. "Flak jackets on, people! I want this bust to go off without any fatalities. But even more so, no officer fatalities, you understand?" All the officers piled into units and vans, headed for their bust site.

CHAPTER 91

WHERE THE HELL ARE THEY GOING?

As Knushka pulled into the slow lane, Kris's face squished up. "Where the hell are they going?" she followed the little clown car. At the last possible second, Knushka's tiny car made a fast right turn crossing the double white lines to take the exit on two wheels.

Kris's Bronco wasn't able to react as quickly as she passed the exit. The suburban that was following, pulled behind her in the suicide lane. Both threw their vehicles in reverse as several of the following police cars sped past them.

Backing up, both vehicles took the exit Knushka had taken.

What had this FUBAR caused? Kris wondered. Did we lose them? Kris began to panic as she now followed the Suburban. Not being able to see around the damn black on black government vehicle, she began to panic.

CHAPTER 92

RUBBER LEGS

Taking the exit on two wheels, I smiled and clapped, "Oh my God, again!" I yelled to Knushka, who had seemed to have lost some of his jovial personality.

After heading down a secluded road for a mile or so, Knushka pulled up to the only place we had seen.

Stepping out of the car, Knushka came to open my door. As we stood staring at the building, Knushka asked, "What is BACKDOOR meaning?"

I shook my head as he hurried us inside the bar.

"We're not open," said a short thin man with a handlebar mustache wearing a pair of leather chaps and a cowboy hat.

"We need sanctuary," Knushka told him.

"This ain't a church, comrade," the man told him.

"And I am not asking," Knushka pulled out his 40 cal.

"That's cute," said the chaps man, as ten other men sitting at a table pulled their own weapons. "Why don't you tell us why you're here, pal?"

"Officers are coming for me, for her," he pointed the barrel of the gun toward me. "I am very rich and can make sanctuary worth your while."

"You see, that's all you had to say," said mustache guy. "We hate cops...and we love money. We're outlaws," he proclaimed.

"Can I get you two something to drink?" the man turned toward the bar to reveal bare ass cheeks that drew our attention.

My brow furrowed, as did Knushka's.

"What kind of outlaws you are?" Knushka asked.

The man took on a look of absolute seriousness, "We are the G.B.C. gang," he announced, his gang nodding their heads in agreement. "We're drug dealers."

Knushka sat stone faced, as did I.

"I am new to area, what is G.B.C. gang?" Knushka asked.

CHAPTER 93

COMPLICATIONS

"There's the car," Fall said, as his mother pulled into the lot.

Just as they got out of the Suburban, three SUV's and two vans pulled up in front of them, guns at the ready.

All the agents from the Suburban put their hands on their weapons.

His own hand on his weapon, Detective Owens said, "I hope you have permits for those?"

"I'm Agent Linn," said Anya. "This is Agent Fall Linn, Ernie Camp and...I don't know this guy as anyone but Agent Miller," she pointed to the young man who was once her driver.

All of the agents showed badges and Anya explained their current situation.

"We heard the call go out over the radio. We didn't think he'd end up here," the detective shook his head.

"What's going on here?" Fall asked.

"We're busting a...drug ring of sorts," Detective Owens told him.

"Meth, heroin, coke?" Fall asked.

The detective looked almost embarrassed, "Anti-depressants."

Fall's face furrowed. "So now what?"

"I would say we go in full force. These guys are said to be armed, though," the detective warned.

Fall looked up at the sign, "*The Backdoor*?"

"Yeah, you should probably be prepared for this," the detective nodded.

CHAPTER 94

SOMEONE STOP HER

Kris pulled up just as Fall and the other agents were being briefed about what they we about to walk in on.

As she made a B-line for the door, Fall told Ernie, "Stop her."

Grabbing at Kris, her elbow flew backward and cracked him right in the nose. Blood spurted as she connected.

"Dammit Fall," Ernie tried to hold her despite the blurring of his eyes from the impact.

"We're gonna need you to behave," Anya told Kris.

"That's my best friend in there," Kris struggled.

"Yes, and that is a dangerous, armed man who has her, and has taken up refuge with some kind of gang. Your husband says that you work logically, I'm going to need you to do that."

Kris did the bull breathing through her nose again.

"We're just getting an update about the...gang, right now," Anya searched for the word for them.

Kris looked up at the sign over the bar; *The Backdoor*. "What kind of gang is this?" she asked.

CHAPTER 95

THE BACKDOOR

"The Backdoor," the detective began, "is home to the G.B.C. gang."

"And what exactly does G.B.C. stand for?" Kris asked.

"They're the Gay Biker Cowboys," he went silent. "The Salem chapter," he added.

Everyone just looked up at the sign.

"Well, I guess the sign is appropriate," Kris said. "Now what do we do?"

Fall had an idea.

CHAPTER 96

FALL'S IDEA

Fall entered the bar with his hands up, "I'm coming in," he announced.

Met at the door by a guy in chaps, Fall was subject to a search. As chaps man checked him thoroughly, Fall's eyes widened.

"That's a little too much time spent on the package," Fall told him.

"I have to be sure," winked the man who gave Fall an unwanted eye full when he turned to Knushka and said, "He's clean."

Fall shook the image away as he moved to where Knushka sat holding a gun on Grace.

"I'm here to offer myself instead of her," Fall told him, moving closer with his hands held up submissively.

Knushka smiled, "Why I do that? She can testify against me...you have little proof without her."

"We have proof that the packages were delivered," Fall pointed out.

"Yes...to her. Only she proves I ever got package from her. She could have kept, sold, thrown in garbage for all I know. Or at least is how my lawyer will spin with it," Knushka nodded. "If I cannot get out of Country, is best for me...she is dead, no?"

Grace's eyes bulged, "You would kill me, Knushy?" her demeanor almost childlike. "I'm really having a hard time reading men," she shook her head.

"Is not what I want do. You are sweet girl," he shrugged, "but is what I would have to do, to stay out of jail. You understand, right?"

"I understand," Grace said. "I'm not a fan of the idea, but I understand it," her bottom lip popped out in a pout.

The bare-assed-chaps-man piped up, "Wait a minute, you're gonna kill that woman?" he pointed to Grace.

"Like I said, do not want to, have to," Knushka clarified for him.

"Well, buddy, I ain't okay with you killin' a woman," Chaps shook his head as did the other gay outlaw bikers.

Knushka gave them a palms-up, "I did not even think your kind of man, liked woman?"

"Buddy we all have mamas," Chaps said. "How do you think more G.B.C.s are made? Without women, we have no more Gay Biker Cowboys!"

Grace nodded in total agreement with this logic.

"But you are outlaws...you said yourself! You should rally behind other outlaws," Knushka questioned their outlaw code.

"Yeah," Chaps shook his head, "that's a bit out of our range. Killers we ain't!"

"What you mean? You sell drugs?" Knushka asked pointing out their flawed logic of what outlaws do.

"We do," Chaps and his crew nodded.

"So...many people die from drugs," he gave a palms-up. "And is people who deal drugs, who are killing them. Hence, you are killer," Knushka educated them.

"Not us," said a big black man in the crew with long Rick James braids.

"How you mean, not us?" Knushka looked at him like he was stupid.

"We don't deal drugs that kill people," Chaps shook his head.

"What you deal then? Even aspirin has killed! You deal candy cigarettes?" Knushka posed the question sarcastically.

"We push anti-depressants," Chaps said folding his arms across his chest.

"Antydepressants?" Knushka tried to repeat. "Those pills they give to everyone these days?"

"Yeah," Chaps said, nodding his head like he was the shit. "We sure do."

Knushka started shaking his head, "Is stupid."

"It's not stupid," Chaps flared. "There are a bunch of people in this town who are in need of anti-depressants and can't afford health insurance to cover the bill. We," he pointed to his merry band of outlaws, "we're all insured. We each have six doctors that write us each six prescriptions a month. We then sell all the leftover anti-depressants at low prices, so everyone can afford to be happy!"

Chaps' gang all applauded and nodded.

"You are no outlaws. You are '*insurance frauder*' at best. You are stupid," Knushka told him.

"Are you implying that I am stupid?" Chaps asked.

"No implying! Saying! YOU ARE STUPID!"

"Well, them's fightin' words," Chaps said low.

"Well, thank the God, I know you no kill," Knushka laughed at him again. "Is so stupid," Knushka shook his head in disbelief.

"Hey!" Chaps pointed to Knushka, "You don't know what hell these people go through. We live in a state that doesn't get enough sunshine. We get very little vitamin D. Some people have a hard time with that," Chap's eyes were crazed. "We're saviors!"

Knushka stared at Chaps for a moment and blinked several times. "Okay, back to you," Knushka said to Fall. "Let's lay on line, shall we? I want out of country."

"Right," Fall said.

"So now you make this happen for me…and maybe I let girlfriend live?" Knushka shrugged.

CHAPTER 97

DEALS WITH THE DEVIL

Anya had a small listening device, no bigger than an eraser, put into Fall's pocket. From this, she and the whole crew of Agents and officers listened to the conversation inside *The Backdoor*.

Anya knew her son would make a deal to save Grace. She knew her son's first duty would always be to save the innocent. But his desire to save her was on a whole other level. Unfortunately, Knushka knew this, too. Anya couldn't help but wonder if Knushka would honor a deal, should one be given.

The officers sent to bust the GBC figured their bust was secondary to whatever the department was dealing with inside. They stayed on just in case anything got out of control.

CHAPTER 98

WAITING

Kris paced as the officers listened to the conversation. She could barely handle depending on someone else to protect Grace. In her mind; she grabbed the gun no one had bothered to take from her, raced through the doors and shot Knushka right between the eyes. She knew if she had a clear shot, this was exactly how the story would end. The only problem was she had no way of knowing if she did in fact have a clear shot.

The Backdoor, like many bars, didn't have windows. It was more of a big barn. Unless you counted that one at the very top of the building, she thought to herself.

CHAPTER 99

AT THE CROSSROADS

"I am not his girlfriend," I crossed my arms over my chest and looked away.

"Ohhh," Knushka said, giving Fall the *you're in trouble* look.

"Grace...I know you're upset. I know you feel like I wasn't...interested. That wasn't the case," Fall searched for Grace's attention. "I wish I would have told you."

Knushka came to my defense, "She no looks like she wants to talk about it," he shook his head at Fall. "You wish to talk of it?" he asked me.

I made a drunken pouty face, "What does he wish he would have told me?"

"I would have told you..." Fall began.

"No, he talks to you," I told Knushka, still refusing to look at Fall.

"Fine," Fall said turning to Knushka. "Can you please tell her," he sighed, "that I do have feelings for her?"

"He has feelings for you," Knushka told me.

"The reason I tapped your phone...was because...I needed to...hear your voice...your laugh. I needed to know...what you were like," Fall said.

"He admits he has weird desires," Knushka told me.

Fall gave him a look, "Can you not try to interpret my intentions?"

"I call them as they are seen," Knushka gave a shrug.

"Anyway, I saw how you were...who you were. The way you light up when a child looks at you...the smile you get when you see a dog...you hold the door open for others and ask if you can return shopping carts for strangers. The women I have known...are good to people...when they know you're watching them. Like they want you to think they're something they're not," Fall swallowed hard.

My eyes were working their way to his as I listened.

"You...you're a good person and a loving soul...even when you think *NO ONE* is watching," Fall shook his head in disbelief. "I didn't know that this...you...existed."

"Oh, now that is sweet," Knushka nodded. "I see how he sees this in you," Knushka told me and patted my hand. "She is good girl," he told Fall.

"Grace...I tapped your phone, not to keep you safe...but to somehow be closer to the kind of woman...the kind of woman...I wish wanted me. I fell for you, Grace!" Fall whispered.

Tears were pooling in my eyes as I turned them to Fall's. His big brown eyes were sincere and pleading for me to understand. This wasn't the action of a total creeper, but the actions of a man who sincerely cared.

Reaching out my hand to touch his face, I smiled. "But that night when we were dancing...you pulled away from me," I said.

"Oh I think I know why he does that," Knushka began to laugh.

I looked from Fall, who had closed his eyes, to Knushka who sat grinning. Suddenly Fall's cheeks turned bright red. "Oh," I smiled.

Standing, Fall took me in his arms. We held each other for a moment before Knushka said, “We have deal to make Agent Fall.”

CHAPTER 100

A MOTHER'S SMILE

Anya and the men sat listening to what Fall was saying. She couldn't help but smile. She knew that her son, who didn't take love lightly, was in love; the real kind, the one that lasts forever. The one she always hoped he'd find.

CHAPTER 101

ROBIN AND THE HOODS

Chaps and his merry band of whatever they were, sat listening to Fall's confession.

"I hope someday," Chaps wiped away a tear, "someone thinks of me that way."

"What if someone already does?" asked the large black man with the shoulder length braids.

Into each other's eyes, they dove. For the first time they saw that there was more between them than the Gay Biker Cowboy brotherhood and outlaw criminal behavior, there was love.

CHAPTER 102

NOT EXACTLY WITH A BANG

Everyone was so caught up in what was going on inside *The Backdoor* that no one even noticed as Kris skirted the building. Hopping onto the lid of a dumpster, she then pulled herself up onto an overhang and scurried across to the only window she had seen. Everyone below looked lost in whatever deal they were trying to make. But Grace was not a bartering point to her.

Through the window she went, undetected. Dust an inch thick covered everything in sight. As her eyes adjusted to their new view she moved forward slowly. Rickety old beams had the less desired effect of making her feel overweight as they creaked a little under her footsteps.

Through the floorboards, lines of light from below made their way into the attic. Getting into a lying position so she could get a better look, she peered through one of the cracks. There, twelve feet below, sat the strangest band of merry bikers she had ever laid eyes on. She wondered if they could be given a *sex-number* in her book. *Outlaw Gay Biker Love*, would add to her demographic.

On hands and knees she moved onward carefully. A man's voice was getting louder as she went. Finally, she could see someone below her. Lying down on her tummy, she spied Grace and the two others directly below her.

One of the guys sitting with Grace was handsome indeed. This must be the infamous Fall. Too bad Grace didn't get her cobwebs cleaned by that guy, she thought.

The other man; in his fifties maybe, impeccably dressed, salt and pepper hair, and barrel-chested, must be this Knushy guy, she figured.

Now that Kris had eyes on them, what was her next move?

That Fall guy was saying something heartfelt (she could tell by the way Grace was responding), but she was having trouble making out exactly what was said.

Turning her left ear slightly to try and hear Fall over the A/C unit, she was face to face with a huge rat.

Kris's eyes rounded as she pulled her face away from the disease carrier. Grabbing the gun from her waistband, she aimed it at the curious vermin.

"I will shoot your head...clean the fuck off!" she warned it.

Its beady eyes slit, almost like he was daring her. As it took a step in her direction her whole body jumped to get away from the fearless rodent.

CHAPTER 103

SEVEN SECONDS IN HEAVEN

I got to tell her how I feel, I was holding the woman of my dreams and she had locked onto me as well. I was sure now, she felt for me, what I felt for her. For a moment it seemed like everything was going to be alright.

Just when I had almost forgotten the world around us, just before I finally got to kiss her, Knushka aimed his gun and ordered her to sit back down.

"We still have deal to make," Knushka told me.

I was ready to give myself in return for her safety, but Knushka wasn't going for it. Maybe, I thought as I prepared to release her from my arms, maybe...something.

Maybe those guys at the bar would find their balls and attack the bad guy? Then again, Knushka would kill at least one of them if not all of them. They had to know they were in a bad position. Plus, one guy I knew for sure was carrying a pellet gun. What were the chances the not-so-outlaw-gay-bikers were actually carrying anything but BB and pellet guns?"

Maybe the Agents and officers would storm the bar? Fall had to admit again, this would end in a bloodbath if they did. And most likely Grace's blood would be the first shed. I mean, she did make all the difference in the case against Knushka.

I held her close and kissed her forehead. Even *higher-than-a-kite,* she was everything I had always wanted and more. Releasing a long held breath and a prayer, I ached when her body moved from mine.

CHAPTER 104

DIVINE INTERVENTION

Of all the people Knushka didn't want to kill, it was Grace. He had become quite fond of her. But she was his last bartering chip. She could not only implicate him, but his whole syndicate; all of his men, his son, Slovak, Amsel. (Last one was of little concern to him, he thought). She could annihilate his whole empire. She must have seen where the packages were from. It would take them nothing to connect the dots. Maybe, he should demand a plane and take her with him? Then, he could send her back on the same plane once he was safely away from the U.S.A.? Or she could stay, he thought to himself. Spring in Russia was beautiful.

He watched them hugging; what a wonderful couple they would have made. Such a loss, Knushka thought. He almost got a little teary eyed, something he didn't want anyone to see.

"We still have deal to make," Knushka said to Agent Linn.

As the Agent squeezed Grace again and kissed her forehead, Knushka let out a sigh. Love is so beautiful, when not wearing red panties, he thought to himself.

CHAPTER 105

ARE YOU KIDDING ME?

As Agent Anya Linn listened, she thought she picked up on a background voice. The voice wasn't a man's and it said, "I will shoot your head...clean the fuck off!"

Anya had a moment of concern. Were they picking up crossed audio; a death threat coming from someone nearby? She took a look around. Where the hell had the best friend, Kris, gone?

CHAPTER 106

FALL LINN, GRACE FULLY

I was beyond happy as I jumped into his arms. He wanted me! HE WANTED ME! I couldn't stop smiling. And in my still a *little higher than I'd like to be* state of mind, it hit me; I wouldn't have to go through all of that getting to know you stuff...at least I didn't have to tell him all about me, which was the part I hated the most (it was hard to make me sound interesting). His embrace left me feeling wanted and safe...until...

"We still have deal to work out," Knushka said.

I was reluctant to let go of him. I wanted just one kiss, but then I feared that it really would be just that one. Knushka was going to kill me. I wondered if he would at least be nice enough to give me another shot of the serum.

Letting go of him, I took a deep breath and hoped for a scene from *Die Hard*, or any other movie where the good guys live.

CHAPTER 107

MEMORIES OF HIGH AND LOW

Now I know I was *high*, although not quite as *high* as I had once been...but I digress. I was just about to sit back down and find out my fate when...I heard...a cracking sound, overhead.

Knushka, Fall and I looked up to see what was happening above, when here came Kris through the ceiling. Yelling the mightiest of all words in the English language; "FUCK," could be heard for miles around, as Kris crashed down on Knushka.

Knushka tightened his grip on his gun, as Kris rolled off of him. Swinging his hand around, he drew a bead on me. I stared at the barrel as time slowed. Out of the corner of my eye, I could see Fall jump toward me. Closing my eyes, I heard the shot. Crumpling in my chair, I felt searing pain tear through me.

CHAPTER 108

THE FALLEN ANGEL - KRIS'S SWORN TESTIMONY

"Last thing I knew, that huge gray rodent with its pink nose twitching away, was within a beer bottle of my face. I tried to lunge away when he didn't back down from my 40cal. Then...there was a freefall followed by a broken landing. As I spun off of that Knushy guy, he aimed his gun and fired at Grace. Without even thinking, I shot him."

"You are aware of where you shot him?" Agent Anya Linn asked.

"In the bar," Kris answered straight-faced.

"I mean, where on the body you shot him," Agent Linn corrected.

"I was going for his penis...but I missed," Kris grinned and wiggled her little finger at the Agent.

"You only shot the one time?" Anya asked.

"Would have tried again, ya know, the penis shot, if I hadn't been tackled," Kris was matter-of-fact about this.

"And the weapon in question," Anya looked at the previous statement given at the bar, "is your husband's service weapon?" Anya raised her brows.

Kris smiled, "Yep."

"No further questions," Anya tried not to smile back.

CHAPTER 109

CHAPS; OF THE BACKDOOR - FOR THE RECORD

"Well I was just gettin' ready to make my move, ya know save the day, when all of the sudden, that crazy blonde chick came through the ceiling. She landed on the crazy guy who tried to kill that other lady."

"Right," Agent Linn said. "Do you and your gang have licenses to carry your weapons, sir?"

"They're uh, BB guns. But they look real, don't they?"

CHAPTER 110

AT THE HOSPITAL - GRACE; ON THE RECORD

"Hello, I'm Agent Anya and this is Agent Barnes. We need to ask you a few questions if you feel up to it?"

"Sure."

"When did you receive the first package for Dmitri Knushka?"

"Ten months ago, I think."

"How many packages were left in your care?" Anya asked.

"Seven or eight I think."

"All of them were then delivered to him by you?" Agent Barnes asked.

"Yes sir. As soon as I realized he was home, I would take them down to him," I nodded.

"When you were abducted, did he threaten you in any way?" Anya questioned.

"No. He didn't say anything about killing me until later."

"Do you know what he gave you, the shot?" Agent Barnes tag teamed me.

"I'm not totally sure. Something he makes himself."

"Did he at anytime discuss previous illegal activity with you?" Anya took her turn.

"Um...he admitted to killing his wife...and brother...when he found them in bed together," I nodded slowly.

Anya and Barnes shared looks at one another.

CHAPTER 111

RECOVERY

Barnes stepped forward and shook my hand, "If you think of anything else," he handed me a card. "Anya," Barnes said, "I'm going to head out and get Fall's official statement."

Anya nodded as the other agent closed the gap between them. Leaning in, he brushed her check with his lips. When he got to the door, he said, "I love you, Anya."

Agent Anya smiled and said, "I would mourn you, if you died."

My shocked eyes turned to her. "Um, is this...just something Agents say to each other?" I asked.

"No. It's something my family says...when they love someone," she gave me a one sided grin. "My name is Agent Anya *LINN*...I am Fall's mother."

"So...*that's* the kind of AGENT he meant," I said to myself.

"I understand you've recently spent some time with my son," she said.

The no nonsense of this hardened Agent kind of scared the crap out of me. "Um, yes ma'am."

"Maybe...that part about him breaking into your home and holding you hostage for a few days, stays between the two of you?"

It was posed as a question, but how stupid would I have to be to think she wanted any other answer than yes ma'am? So I said, "Yes ma'am."

"And maybe when you're feeling up to it...you'll come for dinner?" she finally smiled.

I let out a long held breath and said, "Yes ma'am."

As I slowly drifted from consciousness, I knew...he loved me.

CHAPTER 112

MY TURN

The last time I got to see Grace, she was higher than a kite and being rolled into surgery, Fall thought. Now I had to wait while my mother took her official statement.

Grace getting shot was the hardest thing I could have ever seen. Trying to keep Kris from firing a second round at Knushka, was the hardest thing I've ever done. Someday, she may forgive me for not letting her kill him.

When my mother came out of Grace's room, she gave me a pat on the cheek. "She's lovely," she told me. "Invited her for dinner some time," mom grinned and kissed my cheek before she walked away. I knew mom was happy. Not just because she finally got her *white whale*, but because she knew I was in love.

Walking into Grace's hospital room, I flashed back; my mother in the hospital bed. A bullet had been removed from her shoulder, too. The only thing missing was the guy sitting by her bed, holding her hand. The man that would love her all of her days, I was that guy.

Grace's eyes turned to me, and she smiled, "Hi," she whispered.

"Hi," I walked over to her. "How are you feeling?" I moved the hair back from her face. Even all looped out on painkillers she was still the most beautiful woman I had ever seen.

"Kind of like I got shot," she grinned.

"I'm so sorry. I'm sorry I didn't keep you safe," I told her and shook my head. The guilt of her getting hurt weighed on me.

"What are you talking about? I was told if you hadn't kicked Knushka's arm, he would have shot me straight in the heart," she said. "You…and Kris," she grinned, "saved my life. Thank you," her eyes began to tear up.

"How much of the conversation at the bar do you remember?" I asked her.

"Some of it is a little hazy," she admitted.

I nodded not sure which part was clear. Did she remember me confessing my feelings for her? Was she just loopy when she jumped into my arms?

"I met your mother. Now I get what you meant by Agent. So I assume you're an Agent, too?"

She changed the subject? This wasn't a good sign, was it? "Um, yes I am."

"She's kind of scary…but in a really cool way, though," she yawned.

She was going out. I could see her eyes rolling around trying to stay focused on me. Maybe now wasn't the time to have this talk.

"Fall, would you mind getting me another pillow? My neck's all cricked up," she tried to stretch.

"Sure," I said and headed for the door.

"Fall?" she said. I loved the sound of my name on her lips.

"Yes Grace," I turned back to her.

She smiled so sweetly, "I just wanted to say…I would mourn you, if you died."

My heart skipped as I rushed back to her side. Taking her face in my hands; staring into those beautiful eyes, I saw it there, I knew. Finally I got to kiss the woman of my dreams.

CHAPTER 113

INTERROGATION

Cuffed to a hospital bed, Agent Anya Linn asked Knushka, "Is there anything you'd like to say for the record?"

He looked down towards his manhood. "I guess lucky. Woman who shot me is horrible shot."

Anya couldn't help but enjoy his childish attempt to defend the size of his manhood to her. Some men never grow out of this, she grinned. "Actually, the woman who shot you carries sniper status."

Knushka looked embarrassed.

"But I guess you're lucky...you probably dress to the other side," Anya threw Knushka's ego, a much needed bone.

"Right, right," Knushka agreed. "Lucky for me."

"So anything else you'd like to tell me?" Anya asked again.

"Knushka smiled, "I say...nothing," he said slowly with a cocky grin.

"That's fine," Anya said and headed for the door. "Oh, by the way, your accomplice, Amsel I believe is his name, he's in holding. In fact, I'm going there right now to offer him a great deal," she smiled. "But I'm sure...he can be trusted not to turn on his boss, right?" Anya left the room with Knushka's horror filled eyes watching her go.

CHAPTER 114

THE DUMBEST

As Anya walked into interrogation room 4, Barnes was in the middle of questioning Amsel.

"This is Agent Linn," Agent Barnes told him.

Amsel sat with his head still cocked to one side. As Anya walked behind him, fear showed in his eyes. Grabbing Amsel by both sides of his skull, she made a quick jerking motion, popping his neck back into place.

"Better?" Anya asked.

Amsel rubbed his neck and began smiling, "Better."

"So what does he have for us?" Anya asked Barnes.

Agent Barnes's eyes rounded. "We were in the middle of a story," Barnes nodded. "Go on," he told Amsel as Anya took a seat.

"How was I to know it would die if I did this?" Amsel showed the Agents his palms then continued, "At least did not go to waste! I fed to mob family."

Anya looked really confused. Did he just admit to feeding the Russian mafia one of the people he killed? Amsel looked almost bereaved, as he let out a sigh. Was he feeling guilt over the kill, she wondered. Anya knew this happened sometimes...a true rush of culpability.

"Take your time," Barnes told him.

Amsel continued, "Knushka yelled to me, "*I no care, just get out of sight. Go fuck chicken*!"

Anya's eyes rounded as she spit her coffee out across the table.

"This guy's pure gold," Barnes handed her a napkin.

CHAPTER 115

THE BOOK

On her favorite daytime talk show, Kris answered questions about her book: '*How Relationships Really Work; Forgiveness by Numbers.*' The book became a *New York Times* Bestseller within two weeks.

Fall Linn and Grace Fully, own a signed first edition of the book and have a chapter written for, and dedicated to them. It's called *The Stalker*, or as other people may know it, #77.

THE END

AFTERWORD

No one was harmed during the writing of this book.

Thank You, to my mother and father for teaching me about *true love* and its *worth*.

Don't miss WINGED
Available Now

After being reincarnated three times, Arianna has no desire to ever return to Earth, even though that means she will remain a wingless angel. But when Ari is requested to go on a very special mission, she cannot refuse.

Her mother from Life #3—the only life in which she ever felt truly loved—was none other than God's favorite creation, Eve. Now, tasked with saving her mom's trapped immortal soul, Ari will have to fight pure evil with the help of the most unlikely of souls, the Fallen Angel himself—Lucifer.

Turn the page for an excerpt from *Winged.*

CHAPTER 1

WINGED

He did say, "You'll know her when you see her." He was right about that. Without a single doubt in my mind, this was her. This frizzy, red headed bitch was the one who ruined my life. Well, one of my lives, I surmised. I can, however, blame her for this life sucking, as well. Seeing as how I would never had to be reborn, if it weren't for her. One part of me, the part that was human, wanted to scratch her eyes out! The other part of me…the part that wasn't human exactly, wanted to slit her throat with my wings.

My name is Ari, short for Arianna, and this is how and why I was born into this world…again.

IN THE BEGINNING…

Just kidding, I love that shit though. Anyway, I was called into His office. Who is, 'His' you may ask? Well, 'He', is the Big Guy, the Head Cheese, the Commander and Chief. No, not the president…GOD! Yeah, you heard me, God. Yes, I call him God. No that doesn't make any of my past religions correct, either. He is called by many names, and do you know what all of those names have in common? They all mean 'God' or 'The Divine' or 'One-True-Something-Something'. So your first misconception will be revealed right now, HE DOESN'T CARE WHAT BY WHAT NAME YOU CALL HIM! Anywho, he calls me into his office, points to a chair and asks me to have a seat.

"Ari," he begins, (he always calls me Ari) "I would like you to go on a Mission of Wings."

He would call you by whatever name you wished, and Ari was my soul name. No matter how many spirits I had had or how many bodies I had occupied, Ari was what, or who, I always came back to, and that was fine by me. I felt like an Ari. Mary Magdalene went through a phase in the 80's (the 1980's), where she wanted to be called BIG MAMA M. And of course, that is exactly what we, and God called her.

Back to it, misconception number two: Some humans are under the impression that when you die, you follow a white light to Heaven then Saint Peter looks you up on a roster, like you're in line at a night club. You are led through the red ropes, and then given your wings. They are wrong.

You don't get your Wings until you have gone on, and successfully completed, a Mission of Wings (M.O.W. for short). In truth, most souls in Heaven didn't have their Wings yet. The Winged, as we call them, sometimes acted superior to those of us Un-winged. But never in front of God if they know what's good for them. Truth is, he loves us all equally, and has a 'No Bullying' policy that must be strictly adhered to, or the person is schooled.

I watched once as he un-winged and re-birthed an Angel who got a little too big for said wings. In his outdoor voice, which we so seldom heard, he said: "Wings shall not be retained by one who is so clearly unworthy of wearing them." We all winced as he made his decree. The man was to be reborn... in Africa... as an Albino. Like I said though, schooled!

God pointed to a dish sitting on his desk, "Nut?" he asked.

I shook my head, "No, thank you." He did love his nuts, I thought.

"I would like you to go on a Mission of Wings," (but of course, you've already heard this part) "How well do you remember your mother, Ari?"

I had only been in three bodies since the beginning of my soul's creation. It doesn't sound like many, I know. But they had been more than enough, as far as I was concerned.

My first life had been in China around 200 and something, B.C. I was a Priestess at The Temple of the Moon. In saying that, I was considered a child of the gods and was fostered in the 'house of the gods', from the moment I was born. No human could claim me as theirs, so I never had an Earthly mother. As a child of the gods, I was trained to know every plant, herb, berry and tree, for protecting, healing and killing. Taught to battle with swords, axes, stones, sticks and daggers, I was educated in what would now be known as, 'The Way of the Assassin'. In short, I was a badass.

One beautiful starry night, I was at the Pool of Enlightenment when marauders broke through the gates of our mountain top retreat. My sisters were under attack as the men were set on raping and slaying my fellow priestesses. I remember calling my breath to calm itself, as I pulled my sword over my head and took my stance. Within moments I left a slew of dead men at my feet. But I could see more were coming. I had no doubt in my mind, that I was not long for this life. No matter, I would not let my sacred virginity be taken. As a large group of bandits ran toward me, I put the tip of my own sword to my stomach and yelled in my ancient tongue, "Only in death may you take this body." I ran the blade through, crumpling to the ground. It was all very dramatic. But, the joke was on me. Turns out, rapists don't seem to care so much if you have a pulse or not. And that one guy, who did that thing to my corpse? Well, I asked God if I could haunt his sick ass and he had agreed that what had been done to me was a haunt-able offense. And as a virgin, I did die.

Next life…'A Vestal Virgin': Are you noticing a theme yet? I was made a Vestal Virgin in the year 25BC, at the ripe age of six. Usually, in order to become a Vestal, both of your parents must be living, but my mother had died birthing me. My father was a high born, very rich, muckety-muck, who had me placed as a Vestal despite the rules. I was never to know my mother, or him, for that matter. I was raised in the House of Vestals, educated and untouched.

Our job as Vestals: Keep the Sacred Fire (a tribute to the Goddess Vesta), burning at all times, care for sacred artifacts, collect water from the sacred spring and keep 'the wills' and 'testaments' of the rich and powerful of the time. After 30 years of service as a Vestal, your life suddenly becomes your own. You're given a pension and allowed to marry or own land, whatever you choose.

36 years old, made me a little long in the tooth for those days, but still attractive enough (still had all of my teeth). What I was looking forward to more than anything else was losing my sacred flower. I had heard women speak of it like it was a mind altering drug. I had no desire to marry, even though I would be highly placed. I had 'belonged' to 'someone else' long enough. My plan was to walk down to the local watering hole, find an attractive man and ride him like I was trying to break a stallion. Yep, that was the plan.

The day of my long awaited freedom dawned, and I was ready to be my own woman. The other Vestals, who were like sisters to me, had been given leave to throw me a goodbye party of sorts. I had a little too much wine at said party, but still began my journey down the road to the ale house. I stumbled and staggered, but was set on my goal. I covered one eye with my hand to stop the alcohol induced double vision. But I'm afraid I was more focused on my goal than the road as I fell into a deep hole being dug for a privy. My last word was, "Shhhiiiiiittt!" and as a virgin, I did die.

So, I guessed the Big Guy was referring to life number three.

I had asked him before about my mother, to which he had said, "In time, child." When he said things like this, you knew not to push. But she had occupied my mind on more than one occasion, and I didn't understand why I never saw her in Heaven, or whatever name you call it by.

So today! I thought. Today I find out what became of my mother.

"So Ari, how well do you remember her?"

It was like asking if I remembered the smell of rain or the most beautiful sunrise I had ever seen. I remembered the scent of her hair as I lay curled up in the nook of her shoulder, regaling me with stories of long ago. I remembered skin whiter than fresh snow and hair as black as a raven's wing. She would dance and twirl with me in her arms. When she sang the Angels themselves made no sweeter sound. And I was loved.

"I remember everything about her," I replied.

God nodded at me with a knowing look. "Well Ari," he began, "Do you know what immortals are?"

I furrowed my brow. "Immortals?" I questioned with a grin. Was he messing with me? Sometimes he did that. I knew what the word meant, of course. And, I knew that humans suspected, and even fantasized about the possibility of Immortals. But no one in Heaven believed in their existence.

"In the beginning...,"God started.

There it is, I thought.

"I created two souls. You would know them better as Adam and Eve."

My jaw dropped. I took a moment to let the thought sink in. Finally I blurted out, "You mean Adam and Eve were real?"

God nodded at me, "Very much so."

"And the Garden of Eden? Was that real, too?"

Again God nodded. "But…not the way people believe."

I just stared at him and waited for him to elaborate.

"I hadn't made any other humans," he said, doing a palms-up. "By the time I did, Adam and Eve had been alone on the Earth for thousands of years. They seemed to be unhappy, even exhausted with each other. I figured they needed something new, so finally… I gave them genitals."

I avoided eye contact at this point. It was an unfortunate truth that I was somewhat obsessed with the thought of intercourse, even more so after talking to Cleopatra.

"Well, they woke up one morning and each had their very own, completely separate parts that were totally compatible when joined," he told me.

"So, at first you made humans without, umm, reproductive organs?" I asked.

"Well truthfully, when I first gave them genitals, it was without the ability to reproduce. Sensation only, but then Adam and Eve never stopped...you know."

I nodded, very sure of what he meant, and a little jealous.

"Then, I decided to make more people so Adam and Eve would have others to talk to. Maybe keep them from, well, you know, all the time. I wanted humans to be able to reproduce without me having to spend so much time overseeing their creation. That's how sex organs became reproductive organs. I had an exact blue print of how I wanted them to be made, and even appointed an Angel to oversee creation. I know you've heard of him," God's bushy grey brows lifted.

I raised an eyebrow back. I couldn't even imagine.

"Lucifer," said God.

I had in fact heard of Lucifer. I had also heard all the Christian stories about he, and God's falling out. How he had once been an Angel, cast down for wanting God's power, and so on. Turns out, it was nowhere near the truth. It was one of those, 'Not quite', things.

"When I left him with the blue print, there were specific steps that needed to be followed. Several thousands were made according to the plans I had given Lucifer. Each was to be made, given reproductive organs, and a soul. All would be made from souls I had already created and were in Heaven. They would be born as humans."

I nodded, believing that all humans were made from pre-existing souls.

"A few hundred years or so passed, with the blueprint being followed to a tee. When I checked in, all was running smoothly. I was busy making new plants, oceans, animals, trees, and ridding the Earth of one of my earlier creations that wasn't quite working out. I didn't want to just annihilate these creatures, so I let most of them live out their lives and simply took away their ability to reproduce. It wasn't long before all of those souls were back in Heaven."

"So at some point, souls in Heaven were used for animals, and such?"

"Still are, in some cases."

"Huh," I nodded at this new piece of info. "So what happened? With the humans and Lucifer, I mean."

"Well, Lucifer became bored with his job. And rather than talk to me about it, he got sloppy. See, the whole point of giving the humans a soul, was that Heaven would always pull the souls back when they became increasingly homesick, got very old in their bodies, and so on. Lucifer became so sloppy in fact, that several thousand humans were born without souls, but with reproductive organs. Now here's the kicker, people born without souls, would find each other, like a magnet, and reproduce. And when two people without souls reproduce, guess what they breed?"

I thought I was following well enough to answer, but God cut me off.

"More humans without souls," he answered.

I was really glad I didn't reply. That wasn't my answer.

"So," he continued, "It became a cluster. I asked to see the roster and was shocked. Half of the people created, had no souls. I had set it up that people would be created through intercourse. Following would be a long incubation period, after which the female, who I had given the hole to, or slot B in the diagram, would birth a miniature human."

He saw the look on my face and told me it was okay to ask, so I did. "Why did you make birth painful? Not that I would know but I have been told that it is by far the worst pain ever, almost unbearable. And I was around during the time of human disembowelment, not to mention…being hung and set on fire," I said, raising one eyebrow.

"You really need to let that go, Ari," he said. "The reason I made it painful, was so women would love their children."

I stared at him in confused silence.

"You see, Ari, I made women and men polar opposites. If a man goes through hell, he must kill whatever threatens to kill him, he is a conqueror. If a woman goes through hell, she gives ultimate love to anything that is designed to destroy her, but cannot. She is a survivor."

"Okay," I said, trying not to call BS on God.

God broke out laughing, "I knew you wouldn't buy that one, Ari. The look on your face is priceless." He laughed so hard, he snorted. After he calmed down a bit, he said, "Cut and dry, I gave women a higher pain tolerance. Men, with the pain tolerance I gave them in the original blueprint, well, they would die. Therefore, only a woman's pain threshold was strong enough. I did tinker with some 'A sexual' animals…but it just seemed…lonely," he shook his head. "Anyway, men see this pain that a woman goes through, then he, and the child love her more. He would see her, the weaker sex," he grinned, "as *equals*. Or at least that's what was supposed to happen. The truth is childbirth is the ultimate sacrifice of women."

Great in theory, I thought, remembering how horrible women were treated in my days and ages: Raped, second class citizens, was not what God had planned.

"Anyway," he said, "So the whole human species was all messed up. Humans were being born at a miraculous rate, more humans than I had souls. This posed two problems. One, Soulless people were creating more Soulless people. And two, humans born without souls had no memory of Heaven, or how these souls had known, respected, and loved each other throughout time. All of the souls were connected to each other, bonded. These new Soulless humans had no bond to anything or anyone. This leads us to the biggest problem with the Soulless…no conscience."

Was God saying that my mother was a Soulless human? He could read my thoughts, so a question not asked was still answered.

"No Ari, your mother was not 'Soulless'. When I called out Lucifer on his incompetence, he explained that he had tried to send souls to the Soulless. But as I already stated, more humans than souls was the start of the problem. He then tried various methods of wiping out large groups of people at a time, but only succeeded in wiping out Souled, and Soulless, alike. No doubt you've heard of the Helike earthquake in 373 B.C. and the Minoan Eruption in 1645 B.C. I was horrified. My precious souls had been subjected to horrors. And then, of course, the rumor was started that I was an angry, vengeful God. That I not only let these things happen, I made them happen because I was, I don't know, petty?" He threw his hands up in the air.

I was still confused and I knew it showed.

"Sorry, back to your mom. So, Lucifer, realizing that this

wasn't working the way he had hoped, found Adam and Eve and used the power I had given him, not meant for such things, I might add, to make Adam and Eve immortal. This wasn't his intention exactly. He thought he was duplicating their souls, since I had given him the ability to create life. He then, would put them into the Soulless. If he did that, then he could use them to create more souls and I would never know about the whole soulless fiasco he had put in motion."

I still looked confused, I'm sure.

"See," said God, "I gave every soul a gift. Some can sing or have musical abilities. Others can communicate with animals or understand universal secrets. Still others are peace bringers, have healing hands or are muses for things like love, music and art. Everyone was given some form of magic. But Eve, she was my first female creation."

He smiled when he spoke of her, I noted.

"To her, I gave every talent, every ability, every blessing, and every gift. Lucifer knew this, and thought if he took one blessing, for every soul he tried to create, she would be nothing more, or less, than a normal being. No harm, no foul, so to speak. He was wrong. No one else can take away a blessing or gift I have bestowed."

I nodded, wondering what gift I would be reborn with.

"So, I had given Lucifer the power to create humans, along with a few other gifts." I nodded, in understanding. God continued, "Without understanding what he was doing, he magnified her gifts, until she became immortal."

My eyes grew wide.

I wondered how God could not have known such a thing, especially with the whole 'mind reading' thing.

"I didn't feel the need to read minds until then," he answered again without being asked. "And now, it's just a time saver."

I nodded again. I could see how a slip such as this, would change the way God dealt with things.

"So now, Adam and Eve were immortal. I had to have a talk with them about what this meant. We met at a little outdoor cafe in Sumeria: great food but way too many flies. I still wonder why I created them. Have you ever looked at one close up, Ari? Really, they are magnificent considering the scale in which I was working, but I digress. Anyway, I told them the situation and gave them two choices. I could take them back home and never would they touch Earth again. Or they could stay on Earth through generation after generation and live immortal lives. If they chose to stay, they could not die or suffer any bodily injury until they willed their souls back to Heaven. It was part of this whole 'free will' thing I had started."

I had heard of it.

"Well Adam, after thousands of years, had had enough of the world and had no desire to stay. And truthfully, he seemed a little 'Off' after thousands of years without going home. But Eve, she was adventurous and wanted to see everything Earth and life had to offer. So she had walked the Earth since before time was being kept. In fact, she was alive and well during your first two lives. Weird, huh?"

"Actually, yes, all of this is..." I had no words.

"Mind blowing!" said God, doing the palm motion of a magician revealing a trick.

"At least," I replied. "So what happened to Lucifer? I mean, the Pre-Christians say he rules Hell, but I have always been under the impression that Hell doesn't exist."

"It doesn't. At least not the way they say it does."

I stared at him, just not getting it.

"Ari, Earth is Hell."

"ARE YOU KIDDING ME??? Why would you create Hell?" I asked, forgetting who I was talking to.

"It wasn't Hell when I created it. Once Lucifer did what he did, it became Hell."

"So why don't you just fix it?"

God smiled, "How?"

I stared at him, "I don't know, but can't you...do something?"

"I do, Ari. But short of killing hundreds of thousands of people, I have no recourse. Literally hundreds and hundreds of thousands of Soulless people are walking the world."

My jaw dropped, "That many?"

"I haven't told you the worst part. Over the years, the Soulless learned to better fit into society. And now, they are breeding with the Souled. Their children we're trying to 'Soul' in utero. I have many angels on this particular project."

"How, in the name of...well, your name, did that happen?" I asked.

"They know they're different. Some embrace their disconnection to the world and people around them, becoming serial killers, politicians, and dictators. Others don't want people to know how dysfunctional they are. They become sociopaths, convincing others that they are everything they have ever needed or wanted. Truth is, the Soulless have developed a deep need to be with the Souled. They find their inner light irresistible. Then, before the Souled human knows they are with a sociopath, or a Soulless one, they have reproduced once again."

"And you want to send me back there because...?" I rolled my wrist.

"Your mother's soul is trapped there," God said solemnly.

ABOUT THE AUTHOR

Edith Scheffer is a SoCal native, now blissfully transplanted to the Pacific Northwest. A gypsy at heart with the soul of a witch, Edith has wandered but never been lost. She loves sleeping under the stars and moon, walking in her bare feet, dancing to an eclectic playlist of favorite songs, and proudly parenting her exceptionally fierce and fabulous daughter, Brenna. Edith can mix the perfect drink (bartender by trade), massage your aches away (licensed massage therapist), and entertain you with her many novels (yes, she writes, too!). Her works include The Janie Chronicles, *Winged*, and *Fallen Gracefully*. You can discover more at edithscheffer.net.

facebook.com/AuthorEdithScheffer

goodreads.com/edithscheffer